UNDERTOW

Joseph Michael DeGross

ISBN: 10:0615578527
ISBN-13: 978-0615578521

Hawk Bluff Publishing
3780 Hirst Circle
Lenoir City, TN 37772

www.josephmichaeldegross.com

For Sandra and my children

ACKNOWLEDGMENTS

I am grateful to my readers, Mary Buckner, Mary Bess Dunn, Susan Newell, and Robert Silich for their advice and suggestions with the many drafts of this book. My wife Sandy was instrumental in encouraging me to write stories, and in her copyedit assistance. Selah Saderstrom, an old friend and colleague, helped me to understand the concept of a story in which the story itself forms. Finally, my teachers at Goddard College: Michael Klein, Rebecca Brown, Darcey Steinke, and Paul Selig for teaching me to read critically and learn from the mastery of great writers.

The passing of time is an illusion. There is no time, only the conscious moment lived.

The Author

PROLOGUE

In human memory, perspective may vary. Several people can observe the same place, the same act, but the recollection will only be one's own formulated illusion. For this reason—the illusion—I have changed names, sometimes places, and rarely time-sequences, but mostly, this is how I remember it. The Japanese call this form of recall Shōsetsu. It recognizes variation in memory and the elusiveness of reality. Each life has a story, but recollection of that story causes a distortion in the reality. Parts that seem so important at first glance are only on the surface. Parts with great power are hidden from view like an undertow in the sea. An undertow can be dangerous, but only to those who venture into the water, unaware. Any current can be used to advantage, on or below the surface. One needs simply be aware of its presence and in what direction it flows.

I want you to look and feel and discover what you might about my life, the irony of it; the wonder of it. I want you to understand my power and weaknesses. Consider how you think I am doing because I am no longer certain of anything. There is still time for me to change, but I don't know if it is necessary or even if I choose to change. I may like who I am and my unique view of reality. I attempt to see below the surface and as dangerous or elusive as that place may be, I am mostly willing to venture into the water.

JUDAS GOAT

JUDAS GOAT

This thing that brought torment to my life, I have a hunch it had something to do with Mary Elizabeth O'Rourke whom I met in junior year of college. Her name still evokes images of plaid skirts, Irish wool sweaters, penny loafers—Central Park on a November Saturday in 1961, snow falling in large marvelous flakes. Or, it can evoke cold hatred because she was more a malignancy than anything else. This was apparent very early in our relationship. Nonetheless, I allowed her to invade my spirit—almost destroy it.

The sweet images are few: Trees are bare. A squirrel spirals down a trunk, jerky movement, tail twitching. He stops dead—he's seen us—turns and races upward on the far side of the trunk so that he is no longer visible. The edges of benches, lampposts, shrubs, trees, rounded off softly by clinging white snow. Hotels on the south side of the park and skyscrapers beyond, like ghosts in gray, are the background of this picture in which passing taillights offer the only color. The world cloaked in snow-quiet.

But this image always gives way to another. The sulphur-like smell of burning bleached hair. The scent mingles with more familiar hospital smells: alcohol, tincture of benzoin, rubber. We are in a little recovery cubical where the nurse has rolled Mary

Elizabeth's gurney. I lean over, trying to comfort her. The cigarette between a thumb and index finger touches her blond hair and there is the softest hiss. A thin blue-gray smoke-ribbon rises and then disappears into thin air.

When Mary Elizabeth awakens fully, she will suffer far worse than what she endured with the difficult labor. So the cigarette is offered to palliate. It is three in the morning of the day our firstborn, who was an accident in more ways than one, died and Mary Elizabeth does not yet know.

Eight hours of serious pain was her first experience with childbirth. She screamed. I expected courage. The pregnancy had not been planned.

"You're a Ross, now," I said, embarrassed by her screams. My expectation was that life would be similar to a Doris Day and Rock Hudson movie. But when Mary Elizabeth weaseled her way back into my life, all of that changed.

At the time I was a third year medical student at Columbia, a city kid, a street fighter, a former athlete. I was an idealist, even a romantic. But the military man within me meant a great deal to me. In hindsight, I might have been, at times, an asshole, but I could contain that, or so I thought. Then there was the cold emotionless side of me. It was my power, but where or how did it originate? Maybe it had to do with a willingness to risk a beating in order to hand one out. I never screamed or wept, at least not on the outside. And this woman, who didn't make a healthy normal child, lied to me. Somehow what happened felt like it was her fault. She should have left me alone after I dropped her to begin

a military career of which she did not approve. It was never my intention to see her again.

By reputation, the obstetrician was one of the best in New York City although he was at Cornell Medical School's Lying-In Hospital, not at Columbia. I took her there because I wanted the best for Mary Elizabeth. It was my job to protect her and our child. The doctor called me aside six hours into the labor.

"There's a problem," he said, "It isn't good. The baby is anencephalic. Do you know what that means?"

"I think so."

"No forebrain," the doctor said. "It won't live and I don't want you to see it. I'm going to sedate your wife because she doesn't need to see it either. He leaned closer to me and said, "In spite of our best efforts and intentions, now and again, things go very wrong." It was a one-physician-to-another comment. He turned to walk away but after several steps must have had an afterthought for which he turned to face me. "All her pain, it's because the deformed head gets the shoulders hung up. Shoulder dystocia," he said. "Part of being a good physician is learning to deal with moments like this," he said. "But then you've experienced worse, haven't you? I sometimes forget what you did before medical school. You're probably tougher than most people can even understand." He turned again and disappeared through the delivery room doors at the end of the hallway.

Nonetheless, I did see that infant who died, because I looked through the small window on the delivery room door, concerned for Mary Elizabeth and this anencephalic baby we made. Mary

Elizabeth was no longer screaming because they'd put her to sleep. The renowned obstetrician lifted our newborn daughter from between Mary Elizabeth's legs and tossed her into a stainless steel sink like organic waste....we were going to call her Addi.

I didn't flinch, but something happened inside of me. Later, when I read about anencephaly in the hospital library, it was clear what the doctor had done—he was doing a kindness—making sure a failure of nature did not survive to cause further suffering. And he was right, his reputation and experience. But Addi was my first born. Having not viewed her specific deformity, only that tiny newborn body from a distance through an 8X10 inch window— chicken wire sandwiched inside of plate glass—seeing her for only a second, airborne toward the sink, hearing a soft thud of flesh slamming into stainless steel, a tiny leg seen over the sink's edge for part of that moment as her little body bounced then settled on the cold stainless. I imagined her dying in that cold basin—a gasp, and another, then still. Could she see or feel any of this? No, no. Newborns cannot see! And I can't remember a thing about my birth. These facts consoled me.

When Mary Elizabeth awoke enough to understand, I told her.

"She's gone," I said. "It's for the best. She was badly deformed— anencephalic—missing her forebrain. She couldn't survive."

Mary Elizabeth's eyes filled with tears and she turned her head away. She made no sounds, flinched away from my consoling touch.

Many years later, a dream rose out of my unconscious.

A lovely young woman stops me as I step off the up-escalator in a department store, (Bloomingdales, perhaps, by the scent of expensive parfum.)

"Daddy, is that you?" A hand reaches out, touches me softly.

I turn toward the touch—recognition. *Addi.*

"Where have you been?" I say.

She holds me so tightly and keeps saying *"Daddy,"* in the *most loving* and *needy* tone. *"I've been with Mommy,"* she *whispers* and in this dream *I think Mary Elizabeth has been hiding her from me.*

(For an instant) *there is joy—that Addi lives*—(but it is) *replaced by sobs* (that I hear before I know they are mine.)

Whatever is left of Addi is in a graveyard somewhere in Pennsylvania. There was no funeral. The undertaker opened a family crypt and placed the tiny body with the misshapen head in with Mary Elizabeth's stepmother who also died an untimely death from something seriously wrong inside of her head. No one was there except the workers who opened the vault. Did they wrap Addi's body in white cotton or place it in some kind of bag? Perhaps they put her in something that resembled a shoe box the way you bury a dead kitten or a turtle. It was a wet cold Wednesday in September of 1965. That same day, suspicions of a godless universe were confirmed in my head. The confirmation came in the form of recalled sounds as I walked back to the hospital from a coffee shop at 68th and Sutton Place—echoes of gunfire and the screams of men shot and slashed, entrails exposed, bleeding out their life in a stinking steamy jungle;

newborn flesh striking cold stainless steel; the cement lid of a burial vault sliding closed.

Pansies were in bloom in cement urns that lined the curb for several blocks. Water droplets sparkled on their tiny baby faces— blue, yellow, black. They were silent, but smiled up at me. And these silent smiles evoked a single thought: any chance for sanity depended on learning to deal with endings, learning to hold on to hope, learning to take charge. Mastering the ability to say "fuck it" and mean it.

MY OTHER LIFE

MY OTHER LIFE

In the summer of 1961, between junior and senior year at college, ROTC summer camp turned out to be more than expected. Long forgotten was the so-called aptitude test or psychological profile given to me almost three years earlier during freshman year at Columbia College. The degree of scathing disrespect, anger and arrogance demonstrated by filling in the name Jesus Christ Almighty on the identification page, and creating patterns with the number 2 lead pencil used to darken circles on the answer sheet, was gone from my recall. Initially, I had refused to even consider taking the test until the psychologist said that my scholarship depended on cooperation. Why that reaction? Who knows? But now, in the office of an unknown Lt Colonel at ROTC summer camp (which they told me was for an important interview) I had no idea that what was about to happen had everything to do with that test.

When the Colonel entered, I stood, snapped to attention and saluted. "Cadet Michael Ross reporting as instructed, Sir."

"As you were," the Colonel said. "Be seated Cadet Ross."

He was tall and thin, probably in his late thirties or early forties. He had a full head of blond hair, thick eyebrows, and a neatly trimmed mustache. The mustache, which extended out past the corners of his mouth, appeared slightly darker than the hair on his head. His eyes were steel cold blue and he had a cleft in his larger than average chin. The name, Taylor, was on his uniform nametag. He stared at me and I returned the look, not blinking. Who the hell did he think he was? Was he trying to intimidate me? No one could intimidate me.

"You think you're tough, don't you," he said. It wasn't a question and so I just smiled at him. "We began paying attention to you after we saw what you did when you took the test the college allows us to give to most freshmen."

I had to think for a moment and then remembered the run-in with the psychologist and the fucking test I would not take seriously.

"So that was a military thing? I don't do psychological profiles, Sir."

"Why not? Something to hide?" the colonel said.

"No. Who I am is my business. Sir," I added the 'sir' after realizing I had not said it.

A brief smile started to form but then he seemed to think the better of it. "Well, here is the deal, Cadet Ross. We need young men who are tough and fearless. Maybe you are and maybe you aren't," he added. "But I'm going to give you a chance to find out."

"Yes, Sir."

"And if you are as tough as you imagine yourself to be, I am going to offer you an opportunity of a lifetime."

"I have no idea what you are referring to, Sir."

"You're not supposed to have any idea. But if you want to move ahead with this, you need to understand several facts. First, nothing we are talking about is for anyone else's ears. Second, if you blab about this meeting to anyone, we will deny any truth to it, and you are uninvited to the party. Get it?"

"Yes, Sir"

"You will be called out of ranks every morning starting tomorrow. You will not discuss where you go or what you do. If asked, simply say you are on special detail."

That was how it began—the other part of my life. Perhaps it was an alternate life in a parallel universe. Sometimes it seemed an illusion. After the meeting with the lieutenant colonel, my daily routine at ROTC summer camp changed. They picked me every day for so called 'special duty' details and I was separated from my fellow cadets. I'd go by jeep or truck or even helicopter to various places on the military reservation in Massachusetts. It seemed there were a few others picked for this special daily duty, but we were never allowed to get close enough to even clearly see faces, no less speak to one another.

There were shooting instructions with small arms, an M1 rifle, an M1 carbine, a forty-five Colt automatic and a forty-five Thompson submachine gun. A few others were on the firing range, but we were separated by enough distance to remain anonymous to one another. My shooting skills were excellent and I earned Expert Marksman status with every weapon. Although the first time I fired the 1911 pistol, I didn't even hit the target paper.

"Oh, that is fine shooting Cadet Asshole," the instructor said. "Maybe if you just put the barrel to your head and squeeze the trigger you won't miss."

"Yes Sir," I said. I did better on the next effort—every shot in the black. It had to do with trigger squeeze and steadiness in the grip.

On another day they placed me in a circle with four sturdy looking young men whom I had never seen.

"Do not allow them to pin you down no matter what," the instructor said to me.

"Circle this motherfucker," one of the four said.

"We'll break his fucking legs and arms," another hissed.

The tallest was about my height, six feet, and he looked like a wrestler or weight lifter. He moved in and threw a punch, which I ducked under and then kicked him in the balls. He folded to the ground. I knew I had to move quickly and use hands and feet to avoid any close contact where they could get hold of me. I had a cousin who taught me karate.

Two of them came at me and I jumped away while kicking one in the mouth with my boot. Blood poured out along with several teeth. The other got a hand on my foot and I fell backward to the ground, rolled swiftly and smashed my heal into the armpit of the arm holding my boot. I followed this with a blow to the jaw with the heel of my right hand. As one fellow fell back from the blow, the other attacker was just getting up and I kicked him again in the balls. And so it went for about ten minutes after which it was noted that my four attackers had two broken jaws, missing teeth, a broken nose, and a separated shoulder. I was sore and bruised, but intact. No one had pinned me down.

There was bayonet training. A bayonet was fixed to an M1 rifle and you ran through a course of rubber dummies sticking them with the bayonet, shouting "Kill, Kill!" the entire time.

After the bayonet work, came the knife work—a more skilled form of cutting. The instructor said stealth and a cold heart were essential to success with a knife. Knife fighting turned out to be one of my best skills.

"You need to be willing to get cut and bleed a little if you intend to kill with a knife," is what the instructor said.

I already had several scars from knife fights during my teen years. A piece-of-shit tried to steal my newspaper money one summer night when I was out collecting for my paper route. I used a garbage can lid to protect myself. The scumbag cut me in two places on my hand and arm before I broke his nose and fractured his skull with the garbage can lid. The police made me go to court, but the judge said it was justifiable self-defense. I was sixteen at the time and that piece-of-shit was twenty. My cousin had been teaching me karate since I was twelve.

On other days the special duty included swimming and fighting in the water to keep some asshole from drowning me. The more they tried to defeat me, the colder and more vicious I became. Being a cold mean prick—protecting myself and causing pain to those who were trying to hurt me was easily accomplished.

Toward the end of the eight weeks of ROTC summer camp, Lt Colonel Taylor and I met again.

"Well, Cadet Ross, I've been told you're not full of shit. So, I'm now going to make you a serious offer. While you finish your senior year in college, we will expect you to spend some training weekends with us. And when you graduate, we will continue your training which will include jumping from airplanes, SCUBA training, some demolition training, as well as learning more refined ways to neutralize an enemy and how to survive under the worst of conditions. If you accept this offer, you will get to spend a month at West Point during your senior year at Columbia and you will be an ROTC honor graduate from your college. As an honor graduate you will receive a regular army commission upon graduation."

This was wonderful news. Career military had been the original plan before my parents convinced me not to accept my appointment to the Air Force Academy. Now I would have the same commission as if I had graduated from a service academy.

"Yes Sir, I accept the offer."

The colonel smiled. "I thought you would."

Because of the high security involved in the work of my new unit, nothing about his training was mentioned to anyone. My training schedule was in my college mailbox each week, and it always coordinated with my other classes and athletic activities. There were periodic letters of congratulation on my performance as a potential honor graduate cadet. I went to West Point as promised and all of the privileges and responsibilities of a first classman were available to me. My class A uniform for attending classes and other mandatory cadet functions at West Point was my own ROTC uniform. All the rules of the academy applied to me and I felt a strong kinship to The Corp, although I was not a part of it and knew I never could be.

At the time I was dating a girl named Mary Elizabeth O'Rourke. She hated the new plans for after graduation. She made fun of the military and its mission. She saw a world where everyone was reasonable and above hostile action. Yet, Mary Elizabeth was not above hostility. She had a manner about her when things did not go her way. She sulked for extraordinary periods of time, and often became passively aggressive with finely honed skill. My mother liked Mary Elizabeth. Mary Elizabeth attended Swarthmore and visited me now and again on weekends. Her family lived in a Philadelphia suburb. Sometimes she stayed in the guestroom at my parent's house in New Jersey.

Mary Elizabeth wanted me to become a physician. She knew Mother's ideas, hopes and plans for her son, and that I certainly was smart enough.

"Now Michael me darling," she'd begin with an enormously affected Irish lilt to her speech, "Ya know you'll n'er be happy fighten in wars. You're a lover me darling boy, not a killer."

At graduation Mary Elizabeth pinned on one of my gold bars, and my oldest older sister the other. I was Michael Ross, second lieutenant, infantry, Army of the United States. There was one week of leave and then it was off to Fort Benning, Georgia to attend jump school. I was not required to attend any basic infantry training. I had covered all of that during ROTC summer camp and on those weekends of 'special' training during senior year of college.

Mother was more devastated than Mary Elizabeth. She wept when we said our goodbyes. Dad seemed committed to the decision and I think he was proud to see his young officer son heading off in the car his parents had given him at graduation, a maroon Chevy Corvair Monza convertible.

The top was down and I was a free man, off on an adventure. I waved without turning around after noticing Mother with an arm around Mary Elizabeth, whom she had invited to our home to see me off. But I wanted nothing further to do with Mary Elizabeth O'Rourke. I thought it would be best for both of us. I even made it a point not to look in the rearview mirror.

MEMORIES FROM THE FAR END OF THE BEACH

MEMORIES FROM THE
FAR END OF THE BEACH

It was the summer of 1948. I was just standing there in two or three inches of water, sea-foam at the edges, and a stiff warm on-shore breeze—Jacob Reiss Park in Brooklyn. My father said no one was in the water because of an undertow. The lifeguards had the red flags flying at every station up and down the beach and they'd blow the whistle and yell at anyone who went in further than ankle deep. I didn't know what an undertow was except that it didn't sound like a good thing.

"Hey kid, don't go in any further. I don't feel like getting wet today and your parents don't need to hear that you're lost at sea. The undertow is strong, kid. You'll drown." That's what the lifeguard with the white stuff on his nose said to me and it reminded me of a movie I had seen where something pulls a girl down into this deep pool somewhere in darkest Africa. It looked like such a small pond, but they never found her. The sea water was cool on my feet that hot July day, so I stayed in up to my ankles, and ran away from any big wave that rolled in after pounding in the surf like thunder. Where does undertow come from and why do lifeguards put white stuff on their noses? You don't know this when you're eight years old.

Back then, we came to the beach on Sundays. We came with my parents' friends from Jersey City and Manhattan. We were from Weehawken, which was in New Jersey and famous for the Lincoln Tunnel, the Ferry, and the duel between Hamilton and Burr.

My parents were unusual. They often screamed at one another. When my mother screamed at my dad, she also punched him if he was close enough and then my dad punched walls and broke furniture. He picked up chairs and tables and smashed them down so they broke into pieces. When my dad broke furniture and my mother was screaming I sought shelter behind the sofa and if my bladder was full, I usually pissed in my pants.

The sofa was my choice because I never saw my dad pick that up and break it. Except for the sofa and the hutch, furniture did not last long in our house. I didn't fit behind or under the hutch. My parents did not seem fond of one another. Why did they get married in the first place? Weren't mothers and fathers supposed to be friends? I don't know where that idea came from—maybe from my best buddy Ed's folks. I never saw them scream or punch. Never saw any broken furniture at Ed's house or in any of my other friends' homes.

Sometimes my mother screamed at me. And sometimes she bled. She said the bleeding was from where I came out of her. She called it hemorrhaging and the word frightened me. When she hemorrhaged she also screamed and an ambulance would come and take her to the hospital.

Sometimes I told her I hated her and I did. It was the screaming and hemorrhaging. I'd bang my head against the wall when she bled and screamed. When she returned from the hospital I'd say I hated her just loud enough for her to hear it and she'd say she hated me, too. But whenever she said that she had a funny smile on her lips and I suspected she was kidding me even though I figured I must have done some serious damage when I came out of her. At the time, I had no idea what the hell I was doing inside of her, anyway.

Since none of my friends ever mentioned that their parents bled, screamed or broke furniture, this led me to conclude that my parents were unusual. Fortunately I did not dwell on this. Certain truths about life and love were unknown to me at this time. Two older sisters protected me from difficult fearful truths. They provided me with books about wonderful magical make-believe places where people were mostly happy.

So I'm standing there, ankle deep in the Atlantic and my oldest older sister comes along with her new husband and asks if I want to walk with them to get an ice cream cone. I love ice cream cones, particularly sugar cones with black raspberry, butter pecan, and mint chocolate chip. If given the opportunity a triple scoop cone with all three flavors will be my selection, but they only have one of my favorites at Jacob Reiss Park—the mint chocolate chip. I'm okay with this and the long walk in July heat to the ice cream stand. I like ice cream and my brother-in-law.

My parents like the far end of the beach. Less crowded is what they say. There are no concession stands at the far end of the beach, so it's about a mile walk to get to ice cream, which like the Atlantic Ocean, is cold. Besides, my brother-in-law says we can walk with our feet in the water. My brother-in-law is smart. He goes to college.

My oldest older sister is a nurse and her new husband was in the war. He fought in Germany, house to house. He was a platoon leader. He tells me stories if I ask. He carried what was called a burp gun—automatic forty-five caliber—he says it sounded like someone burping when it fired is why it is called a burp gun. He was wounded by shrapnel in the arm. He got a purple heart and a bronze star. He is still a reserve second lieutenant. I'm proud of him. I want to be like him.

I like the story of when his platoon sergeant was taking a shit in a doorway and a Nazi tank came around the corner and my brother-in-law told the sergeant they had to get the hell out of there. The sergeant pulled up his pants, shit and all. Still my brother-in-law got hit with a piece of shrapnel from a shell that tank fired, but his platoon knocked out that tank with a bazooka. A bazooka looks like a pipe and shoots a tank-destroying rocket-kind-of-thing.

My oldest older sister and her husband hug and kiss and laugh. It appears to me that, unlike my parents, they are happy. We hold hands, me in the middle, all the way to the ice cream stand.

What if they share fifty-one years together, then he dies of cancer and she becomes demented? She will say when she is becoming demented that she wishes she would have married the doctor who wanted her to run away with him just after she married my brother-in-law. What if she takes pictures of herself and gives them to me because she knows that she is disappearing. What if when my brother-in-law dies of cancer I'll be much older, and a physician, but there will be nothing I can do to save him or my oldest older sister? After my brother-in-law dies, that doctor she did not run away with may send my oldest older sister a locket. He may also send her kind letters and have a wife who doesn't die. My oldest older sister may not die, either. She will sit in a chair in an institution and talk to a stuffed cloth doll. And what if when I visit she will not know me? She will be dead, but not gone. I may look at the pictures from when she was alive for awhile, pictures of happy hours shared, but then I'll stop looking.

So we walk the beach all the way to the ice cream concession. A triple scoop mint chocolate chip sugar cone is my choice. My brother-in-law pays the man. He gets the mint chocolate chip, too. My oldest older sister likes peach.

I call her my oldest older sister because my other older sister is not as old as my oldest older sister. This youngest older sister does not seem to like sitting around at the beach. She sings and plays the piano. She is very smart. Speaks three languages. Translates literature for a living, but would rather be an actress or a singer. She got a scholarship to Julliard for her piano playing but she didn't take it. Mother and Dad were very upset and then they were sad. Of course, Mother screamed and Dad broke a soup bowl against the kitchen wall. It had green pea soup with slices of red frankfurter in it so besides the crash of the bowl slamming into the wall it made a colorful mess. Nonetheless my youngest older sister did not go to Julliard.

What if my youngest older sister never makes it in show business? What if she takes alcohol and Valium and I never know if she found happiness because what if she decides that the rest of us, me, my oldest older sister, my brother-in-law and Mother and Dad all freak her out and she disowns us? Maybe she will stick to the disowning until she dies of cancer from smoking cigarettes. What if she dies when she is sixty and her husband whom I will never know has her cremated and spreads her ashes at Cape Cod? I will think she must have liked Cape Cod. What if after she disowned us she won the fight with alcohol and Valium? And what if when I hear and think these things I will be an older well respected physician and professor of medicine, and still a warrior of sorts, but none of this will help my youngest older sister in any way?

So we are walking back down to the far end of the beach where Mom and Dad have the blankets, the two umbrellas, the very heavy metal coolers, one filled with food and the other with iced tea, and where the wooden folding beach chairs sit under the umbrellas. Each time we come to Jacob Reiss Park we make a long hot portage carrying all of these essentials from the parking lot to the far end of the beach. I do my share of carrying to the far end of the beach, always glad it is not the far far end of the beach because the walk is already long enough for me. Homosexual people go to the far far end of the beach and mostly people who are not homosexual do not go there.

Sometimes the homosexual people put on little plays. When they do that, lots of the people who are not homosexual walk to the far far end of the beach and watch because the plays are funny. Homosexual men play both the girls and the guys in the play. When my dad sees homosexual men walking on the boardwalk toward the far far end of the beach he climbs up over the railing and walks behind them swinging his hips and waving his arms with his hands in an odd wrist-dropped way. My dad drives a truck for a living. He quit school in the eighth grade. He wanted to fight in World War One but he caught typhoid fever and couldn't go.

I know what homosexual means because my mother tells me. She says it has to do with men and women who fall in love with other people who are the same sex as they are. She says they can't help it. She tells me this because I have a friend who may be like that. He plays with dolls. He wants to be the mother. He acts more like a little girl than a boy. I get into fights because of him. Everybody makes fun of him but my mother says I need to protect him. I'm tough in certain ways. So I fight for my friend who wants to play house and be the mother. I fight and get bloody noses and then I wish he would like stickball or street hockey. Sometimes I wish that he wasn't my friend.

My friend who wants to play house and be the mother will learn to date girls in high school, but in college he will fall in love with a fellow. What if at forty-four he will have a fever and a rash and he will call me and ask for help because he will know I am a professor of medicine and a well respected physician? What if I send him to a famous infectious disease specialist but he will nonetheless die from AIDS in six short months? He will ask me once he recognizes that he is going to die what he can do. I will tell him he can die well and courageously and help educate other gay men so they do not contract AIDS. But what if he tells me that was not what he wanted to hear and I will not know what else to say to him even though I am a well respected physician and professor of medicine? What if nothing I can do will save him? And when he dies in the seclusion imposed by his mother who is ashamed of his homosexuality, I will cry on the inside for him and the torments of his life, but I will never allow anyone to see me crying because self-control will be my necessity.

As we return from the ice cream concession and get closer to the far end of the beach, I see my father running toward me waving his arms. He is far away but may be making fun of the homosexuals. As we get closer I hear him screaming. He is screaming at me. There is a crowd around my mother and she is crying. She is screaming and crying worse than I can remember her screaming and crying ever before. As my father approaches I see that he may mean to do me harm. Hiding behind my brother-in-law who knocked out the Nazi tank seems like a good strategy.

My father, while screaming and crying, says my mother thought I was taken out to sea by undertow. Because of my history of stubbornness they thought I went in too far and the undertow got me. He says when my mother noticed I was no longer standing where I had been, ankle deep in the Atlantic, the lifeguards actually went out in there catamaran and rowed around and dove down trying to find my body. Then they told my mother that if the undertow got me I wouldn't be found for a long time or maybe never. So now she is screaming and sobbing and even a sympathetic crowd cannot comfort her.

My father keeps trying to get at me and I don't know what he intends to do once he gets those big hands on me. My father used to be a professional boxer. He might break my head. My brother-in-law and my oldest older sister keep saying it is their fault because they asked me to go with them for ice cream and my father says I should have told my mother I was going for ice cream and everyone is shouting and waving hands.

And then my mother notices me standing with my dad and my oldest older sister and my brother-in law and she runs over and hugs me and holds me and cries and says she loves me.

My dad quiets down when he sees my mother hugging me. Then he comes over and hugs me too, but he doesn't stop crying.

What if many years later, my dad will also cry after he has several strokes and can't think or speak in a manner others can understand? Perhaps I will sit next to his bed and rub his forehead and his hair with my hands and tell him that I love him and thank him for being a good father to me and then I will see the tears slowly make their way down his cheeks. I will be a respected physician when this happens, and still a warrior of sorts. I will also be a grateful son because my dad loved unconditionally. But neither respected physician, nor warrior will be able to save him from more strokes, eventual pneumonia and death.

And what if my mother outlives my father by five years but gets cancer and suffers? When she is suffering perhaps she will not scream. She will tell me not to cry for her because she had a wonderful life. "My life was a shining star," is what she may say. Then the pain will get much worse and she will cry out in the night and ask me to help her. I will be a respected physician when the pain gets much worse and being a respected physician is what she will have wanted me to be. I will adjust the morphine drip so she no longer cries out in pain before she dies quietly in her sleep.

We went to Jacob Reiss Park on summer Sundays between 1947 and 1956. We usually stayed until everyone else left the beach and headed for home. My mother and the other women would sit on blankets in the gloaming, umbrellas closed, the men and children often taking one last swim in the Atlantic as long as there was no undertow. That particular day remains clear in my memory.

The water felt warmer as darkness came on. It has to do with the ambient air temperature in the evening when there is no sunshine. My mother and her friends were discussing life, things lost; children, adults, and other things that could be or had been taken away.

When the rest of us came out of the Atlantic and dried off, if there was drift wood, we'd build a fire and sit and think and smile in the warm firelight. Occasionally we'd toast marshmallows. This was when I began to learn the truth about loss. But maybe it isn't a good thing to learn at too young an age—that everything is eventually lost by everyone—that humans mostly find ways to hide this truth from themselves; that they rarely come to terms with what they know—eventually, we lose everything that we love.

"Make sure it's out, and bury the ashes under plenty of sand," the beach patrol ranger would say if he saw the fire and drove over to the far end of the beach. Now and again there might be other firelight further up or down the beach, but always there were the lights of boats far out near the horizon like fireflies hovering over the black water. Back then how those boats found their way home in darkness or why they were out there in the night was unknown to me.

The night they thought I had drowned we did not build a fire or go into the water after dark. There was a big wind. The breakers were pounding and a fresh scent of cold seawater was in that wind. Still, that night, we were the last to leave the beach. It was dark when we packed up and headed for the parking lot, carrying all of our beach things to put in the trunk of my dad's '36 Oldsmobile. As I balanced a folded umbrella on my shoulder and carried a rolled blanket under my arm I walked backwards all the way to the steps that led to the concrete walkway because I wanted one last look at those far-off lights on the horizon and wondered if I would be feeling anything had the undertow taken me out to sea. Do you feel things when you are dead, like the coldness of the sea water? They're all gone now—family and friends who were there the day my mother thought her young son had died.

Years later, I will buy a sailboat. I will remember those lights on the horizon and learn to find my way home in darkness. Sometimes I will anchor off beaches in many different places and when darkness arrives, set the anchor and turn on the masthead light. The boat's halyards, driven by the night's wind rising, will beat a pleasing rhythm against the mast. That hymn of wind and halyards will bring magical memories. Sometimes I will share these nights with lovely young women who often wind up naked in my arms out on deck. And I will make love to them so they sing out like night seabirds, harmonizing with the hymn of wind and halyards.

Now and again, shortly after dark, firelight will appear at the far end of some beach, an orange-yellow far-off-twinkling like a star waiting for a wish. Sometimes I will consider rowing the dingy to shore to see who built the fire, but there will be pounding surf and darkness and so, I will not. Dreams, imaginings, and other adventures will suffice. I'll learn to do what is necessary to remain in control of my life.

DREAMS AND SCHEMES

DREAMS AND SCHEMES

At first I was shy with females, so it took me some time before I would invite lovely women to spend time with me on my sailboat. There were summer loves—brief romances framed by issues of courage, boundaries, and desire. To hold hands or not to hold hands. To steal a kiss or not to steal a kiss. And later, to steal more, beg for more, be offered more. Summer-names: Eleanor, June, Margie, Carol, Nancy, Priscilla, Diane, Lovey. These names and the memories haunt me, and I know why. I missed out on one of them.

And there was Kim Novak. I fell in love with her in 1955 when she and Holden danced in the movie *Picnic*. It was a defining moment for love in my life. I wanted to touch her myself—dance with her myself. I wrote Novak a letter. The letter was not answered, but that character represented what I wanted—a real girl who looked at me the way Novak looked at Holden while they danced.

Lori Ann Quinn was that real girl—or so I believed. She rose out of the fire that Novak started. I wanted to touch Lori Ann's legs and other parts. My friend, Bruce Charles, introduced me to Lori Ann, who was his cousin. At 15, she was wild and wonderful. She kissed hard and with her tongue and jammed her pelvis into mine. I always got hard and she would notice and rub against my erection with her pelvis. I was in love with Lori Ann. We went to movies and to dances and she came to see me play football and I went to see her cheer in her short cheerleader's skirt that showed plenty of her lovely legs. And then she dumped me for an older guy. I think he knew more about how to make Lori Ann happy. At the time, I knew nothing at all about sex play. There were just wet dreams and a book my mother gave me as the foundation of my sexual schooling. Somewhere in my twelfth year, the dreams came. They featured a girl named Wendy who babysat for me when I was seven or eight.

I am naked and erect, hanging on to a flagpole that extends from an Empire State Building window high above 34th street. A female appears in the open window, that babysitter. She reaches out trying to save me. As she reaches I see down the front of her blouse—lovely firm breasts, erect nipples. The girl—Wendy—climbs out onto the ledge of the window and exposes plenty of perfect leg. And when she finally gets a hold on me it is my erect penis she grabs—she smiles and her hand is soft and warm.

And that's when the dream became wonderful—a feeling of release, almost pain but more pleasing, more like rapture and this was what I understood love to be.

The first time Wendy babysat for me my mother asked her to be sure I took a bath. Wendy not only made sure I took a bath, she assisted me in doing so with some very special bathing techniques.

"Did you have a bath today?" she said.

"I hate baths. I don't need a bath."

"Baths are nice," she said. "I can give you my very special bath."

And it's the way "very special" came out that captured my interest. She had long brown hair and nice eyes and a nice mouth. So I went for it. And after that first bath all I could think about was when will she be back to sit for me again.

On her return, after my parents left, she said, "Did you have a bath today?"

And I said, "Nope, no bath today and I'm really dirty."

She took off her clothes and my clothes and we climbed into the tub together.

"I don't think it's clean yet," I said as she stroked away the dirt from my seven year old penis.

"Now you have to wash me," she said and showed me how to stroke away the dirt from where she didn't have a penis.

I cannot remember how many times she came. Her name, her face, lost. I only remember that I didn't like it when she stopped baby-sitting. Perhaps mother figured something out or maybe I spilled the beans—said something about the unique baths and how she would cry out when I washed her private parts. "Oh Yes! Please don't stop—don't stop!" And her full young breasts would jiggle as she cried out and I would touch them because they seemed to call out to be touched, her nipples sticking out hard and calling to me to suck on them, which I did. Maybe it had something to do with the fact that my mother never breast fed me.

Years later when I was having that wonderful dream Mother must have noticed the dream-cream-mess in my bed because shortly after the dreams began, a book appeared in my room. Mother said I should read it because "wonderful" changes were taking place in my body. The book was about sex and making babies and it had pencil drawings that were nowhere near as pleasing as the dream-images and memory-images of Wendy. Making babies came up right away. It killed the joy, ruined the mystery and pure pleasure of the dream. Nonetheless I read the book and learned the ropes. Wow, sticking my erect dick into a vagina! But then what? I did not connect the 'wet' part of the dream with the sticking-in-of-the-penis. I thought perhaps the "ejaculation" word in the book referred to urinating into the vagina since urine was the only thing I actually considered as coming out of a penis at the time. I didn't connect the mess in the bed with the 'ejaculate' word. So, despite the books clinical approach to orgasm my ignorance remained intact.

One afternoon sitting in the parlor with my father, I had to urinate. I stood up and said I needed to go to the bathroom to ejaculate. Dad looked at me for a long moment and then said I shouldn't announce it that way and I said it sounds better than saying that I had to go piss. He looked at me again with an expression I was unable to translate.

I did not figure out the connection between the wet dreams and masturbation for quite some time. I didn't put two and two together until several months after my thirteenth birthday when I had a coming-of-age conversation in the schoolyard. An older kid challenged my knowledge regarding the word 'fuck.'

"So, Ross, you're so fucking smart (which I knew I was)," he said, "What does fuck mean?"

Now, I had him. I'd read the book. "It means sticking your dick into a vagina."

"Yeah, and then what?" he said.

"You push it in and out like a tire pump handle," I said, laughing, clapping my hands and working my pelvis like a pile-driver.

"Yeah, yeah," the older kid said, "But then what do you do?"

"You mean the pissing part?" I asked.

I paid for that comment for years. Friends said I'd never get a girl to make love to me more than once. They warned girls not to go out with me because I had a water problem. They asked my dates if they knew how to swim and then cracked-up. The girls would look at me as if my friends were crazy. I never explained the joke but still I worried about pissing accidentally should I ever be lucky enough to find a girl who wanted to have sex with me—until Dr. Charles, who was Bruce's dad, explained that it is not possible to piss through an erect penis. I was greatly relieved.

So, I came of age slowly, and afflicted with an incurable disease, a serious problem—I was a romantic, believed in Santa Claus until I was almost ten. One of the older kids in the neighborhood mentioned that Santa Claus was not real, only a lie perpetuated by parents. I threw a slate roofing tile at him which caused a laceration on his head that required twenty-three stitches. I didn't like it when anyone tried to alter my expectations or imaginings.

It never occurred to me as I grew into manhood that the Holden character and the Novak character in *Picnic* might not make it. There was no difference between passion, sex, and love. Humans knew by instinct whatever was necessary to know about love. Love was Lori Ann Quinn's face, her legs, her smile, her pelvis pressing against my stiff dick. Love was an orgasm inside of Lori Ann Quinn—real or fantasized.

Yet, in spite of my romanticism, it occurred to me that emotions were a problem because they distracted from logic and reason, the application of which should assure sound decision-making, perfect love, and remaining in control. My mother and my youngest older sister were emotional. Their behavior could become distracting, embarrassing. My oldest older sister was not like that. She always seemed calm and in control. Calm and in-control became my golden rules. I would find love logically. Emotions needed suppression.

MOLDING A MAN

MOLDING A MAN

But there was more to my formative years than just girls. Have I mentioned Bruce at five and his dolls and my fights because of him? It was hard duty being Bruce's friend because he loved those goddamned dolls. But Mother said Bruce needed a friend and I don't know why she said it. Maybe she knew that Bruce was always being picked on or maybe she wanted me to be friends with a wealthy well educated family. Bruce's grandfather owned a coat factory and his father was a physician.

"You're the father and I'll be the mother," Bruce would say.

I hated that game, but Mother told me I had to be polite and sometimes play what Bruce wanted. I liked stickball or playing the Lone Ranger. I wanted Bruce to be Tonto. I also liked playing war, which is what we were doing when we found the air pump in the vacant lot down at the end of Dodd Street. Three or four of us were pretending to sneak up on Jap soldiers when the air pump showed up half buried in weeds and beige sandy soil in the lot we called Iwo Jima.

We were excited—checked to see if the pump worked—it did. Bruce, who never played the war game, was sitting in the grass dressing one of his dolls. He saw the pump and seemed

41

immediately interested. He came up with the idea of placing the pump nozzle up his ass.

"Pump air into me," he said. "I'll bet it will cause extraordinary farts."

Bruce used a higher level of language than the rest of us. It was his mother. But big farts sounded like a fantastic idea to ten and twelve year old boys. I was given the job because Bruce was, after all, my friend. I tried to make minimal contact between his asshole and the nozzle but no air was getting into Bruce's bowel. Bruce insisted I shove it in further. One of the twelve year olds, Kenny, grabbed the air pump out of my hands. He spit on the nozzle and shoved it into Bruce's asshole. It didn't look nice and Bruce gasped before he smiled.

"Now pump," He said followed by a grunt. The black hose was connected firmly to his butt hole.

Kenny pumped.

"Pump until I say stop," Bruce said through clenched teeth and stalled breathing.

One fart lasted thirteen seconds—one-one thousand, two-one thousand. I counted.

We did the pump thing for weeks—ran home after school to get it. Mostly it went up Bruce's ass because he insisted. If we didn't use Iwo Jima, we used the alley between my house and Mrs. Grogan's, our nice-old-lady-neighbor.

One Saturday afternoon Mrs. Grogan walked out the front door just after we pumped up Bruce. She heard the last five seconds of a record-breaking fart, but then smelled the shit, which Bruce accidentally lost along with the eighteen seconds of air he expelled.

"Oh my," little Mrs. Grogan said as she walked into the alley following the unpleasant smell. She saw the air pump in my hands, Bruce's bare ass, and the brownish foul-smelling slop on the ground. She began screaming for my mother as she retreated, moving faster than I thought possible for her bowed old legs. She was holding a scented lace-bordered handkerchief over her nose. Mother ran from the house, saw Mrs. Grogan in distress and stopped for a moment to listen to Mrs. Grogan's words which were exiting her mouth in spurts and stops. Then Mother marched into the alley like a charging rhino. She stopped for only a moment to process the picture and then took the pump from my hands. She ordered me to hose out the shit and insured I did it correctly by watching from the bathroom window in our house where she was supervising Bruce in his personal cleanup.

That night I received a long lecture about putting things into orifices, about inappropriate behavior, and about taking advantage of friends. "He wanted us to shove it up his ass," I said. "It was his idea."

"Don't interrupt me," my mother said. "And don't use that kind of language when you are speaking to me."

"What language?"

"You know what language."

"I don't know what language."

"The 'A' word," she said.

"Are you serious? You don't want me to use the word ass? It's a perfectly acceptable word."

"Yes, if you are referring to a donkey—a jack-ass, which is what you are being."

"See, you used the 'A' word," I said. She slapped me across the back of my head. It didn't hurt.

My father stayed clear and I knew why. I heard him laughing and Mother getting angry over it when she told him of the escapade in the alley.

"Bodily orifices are made for things to come out of not go into," Mother said.

"Oh yeah, what about eating?" I said, "And why do you give me enemas?"

"So you will not be sick. It's different when a doctor prescribes it," she said.

"We put food into our mouths and nose drops into our noses. Does a doctor prescribe that?" I asked.

"We're done talking about this," Mother said. "If I see another air-pump in your hand that isn't connected to a tire, you won't go out to play for six months."

My mother had great credibility in this area of threats. She had already kept me in for several months after I spoke some smart-ass words to a fourth grade teacher and was sent home from school. I told the teacher she couldn't control a classroom full of fourth graders if her life depended on it. I also told her she was a crab because she was.

I didn't like anything shoved up my ass, but Mother was in the habit of giving me enemas for my high fevers when I was very young. Fortunately Dr. Charles discovered the cause of my fevers after he returned from Burma. It was a rare infectious disease— Undulant Fever—contracted from drinking raw goat milk, which was one of my father's ideas of humor when we visited Uncle Angelo's farm in New Brunswick. Dad would pull a goat's tit and shoot the warm sweet milk into my mouth as I crouched below the goat's belly trying to provide a target. He didn't know the risks. The disease is also called Brucellosis. Dr. Charles cured me with Sulfa drugs and a new kind of antibiotic called a tetracycline. No more enemas, which were prescribed by the fat little pediatrician who never did diagnose the cause of my fevers but just shot me full of penicillin whenever I had a fever. This ended the episode but did not cure the illness.

I think the sight of me convulsing on one occasion produced Mother's extreme and phobic use of enemas to lower my temperature. Maybe that convulsion played a role in the modeling of my unique brain.

On Bruce's 14th birthday I learned something new about him. His mother gave him a special birthday party. When she was ready with the cake and wanted all of us in the dining room to sing *Happy Birthday*, Bruce was missing.

"Michael dear, would you find Bruce for me," his mother said. I could always tell by the tone of her voice when she was annoyed.

I climbed the back stairs to the second floor, walked past the dumbwaiter in which, when younger and smaller, I used to ride between floors in Bruce's parents' home. Bruce's bedroom was at the end of the hall in the front of the house. Perhaps he might be in his room because he loved board games and the playroom adjacent to his bedroom contained dozens of them. I called his name as I opened the bedroom door. Bruce was lying on his bed with Warren whose erect penis was in Bruce's mouth.

I think I said, "Oh shit," and then added, "Your mother needs you down stairs to blow candles—blow out candles." I closed the door and ran back downstairs. Bruce and Warren appeared in a minute and Bruce had a silly smirk on his face.

Several weeks later the subject of blow-jobs came up, again. Bruce and I were hanging around trying to figure out something to do on a Saturday morning.

"Let's go to the schoolyard and play stickball," I said.

"I don't like stickball. Want me to suck your stick?" Bruce asked.

I was surprised by the question but actually gave it serious consideration. Pubescence for the male is a lonely place. The wet-dreams had stopped, the novelty of showers had worn off and I was looking for some alternatives to coming in my own hand. Well, that's not entirely truthful because I don't think I ever tired of jerking-off. My penis became sore from it—developed abrasions from it. I attempted to suck my own dick. The idea struck me when I was watching Bruce's boxer, Fred, lick his balls. Then I watched a contortionist on The Ed Sullivan Show place her head between her own legs and I was certain that if a person could get their head into that position they could suck their own dick. But inflexibility did not allow me to get to my own dick. So Bruce's sucking my dick sounded like a plausible alternative to my hand, and therefore the question demanded serious consideration. I tried to picture it—my dick in Bruce's mouth—as I leaned against the porch railing.

"Well," Bruce said, "If you take all day to answer you're going to hurt my feelings."

I thought about Novak—my dick in her mouth—then about my dick in Bruce's mouth. The mental picture kept rejecting—my dick in Bruce's mouth. I could still see Bruce with Warren's dick in his mouth. But my dick in Bruce's cousin Lori Ann's mouth—that worked for me. The picture faded in and out because back then nice boys didn't think of nice girl's with dicks in their mouths. At least that was what had been taught to me in certain indirect inferred ways. Nonetheless, my penis was not going into Bruce's mouth.

"Look, I don't think I'm going to like it," I said.

"You'll never know until you give it a try," he said. "You don't have to look down. Imagine Kim Novak is sucking your dick."

"No, I've thought about it and it won't work. How about you get Lori Ann to suck on my dick?" I said.

Bruce laughed. "Oh you dirty little boy," he said. "We'll see what can be arranged."

And that was the last time Bruce ever made a pass at me. There were times when I wondered if maybe I had some homosexual tendencies in me because of my friendship with Bruce or my mother shoving that enema nozzle up my ass or my shoving the air-hose up Bruce's ass. As I got older and wiser I occasionally thought I might be a set up for becoming a homosexual. My father mistreated my mother. I was a momma's boy to begin with. Why would I want Bruce as a friend? But when I occasionally wondered about the idea of being sexual with another male, it didn't feel appealing. It seemed weird and undesirable, like imagining eating worms and caterpillars instead of steak and lobster.

Years later a psychiatrist friend suggested it was this experience with Bruce and the questions it caused me to ask myself that explained my unusual freedom from homophobia, which affects most males in my generation.

I didn't understand Bruce's attraction to males but it was his way and it would cost him his life. Many times in my wenching debauchery as a twenty something and thirty something I had to see a physician for a shot of penicillin which was curative. When

Bruce contracted AIDS, there was no cure or even treatment. He died in his early forties.

Did defending Bruce from bullies help develop my toughness? Maybe everything has a purpose. Maybe, things are connected in ways we don't understand. My mind is inclined to deconstruct my experiences, analyzing them along with my reactions and behavior. In this manner I learned to see things that other people do not—things about life and death. It takes brutal honesty to see the truth.

ACTIVE INGREDIENTS

ACTIVE INGREDIENTS

When I was very young, four or five, my father taught me to read the Sunday comic strips in *The New York Sunday News* and *The New York Sunday Mirror*. Mother was excited about my learning to read so easily. She bought me my first book which I read myself; *King Arthur*, Garden City Publishing Company, New York City, 1932.

I embraced the story, the fellowship of the Round Table, the quests of the knights. I daydreamed between sentences—saw the beauty of Guinevere and The Lady of The Lake. Imagined myself on a great black charger, riding to the rescue of damsels in distress, having my own quest—to end all evil and right all wrongs. The book, however, did not address rumors I learned years later about Lancelot and Guinevere—it neither spoke to love's complications, nor that the grail was never found. It only hinted that Arthur died lonely and sad—his body taken off by The Lady of The Lake so as to extend the magic.

Nonetheless through this book the ageless battle for the good and against evil became known to me. The Second World War was going on in Africa, Europe, and the South Pacific as I read and re-read the pages of *King Arthur*. Other wars would soon follow where it seemed to a romantic young man that clear lines were drawn between good and evil.

I saw myself a modern knight. The horse and lance gave way to fighter planes and machine guns. I wanted to fly. Knew all the WW II aircraft—had a card-set of every fighter and bomber flown by every nation involved in the war. The British Spitfire, the US Army Air Corps' P51 Mustang and P38 Lightening, the US Navy's Corsair were my favorites. Carrier landings and aerial combat were my goals. Lori Ann Quinn was my Guinevere. Attending Annapolis or West Point were the dream-plans. At the time, however, I did not know of my mother's unfulfilled dream-plans and how they would quietly and irrevocably infect my choices.

So, back to Lori Ann—I was overcome with love. I called it love—knew it as love. We worked out a plan because we needed more of each other than we had been able to get. Lori Ann would be a house guest at my home for the Spring Ball—spend the night. My dad would chauffer us to the dance because I was only sixteen and not old enough to have a drivers license. Lori Ann would sleep in the guest room, which was down the hall from my room, my grandmother's room in between.

Grandmother did not hear well and slept soundly.

Even though we never spoke specifically about this plan, I wanted to believe that Lori Ann was thinking what I was thinking—needing what I needed. Why else would she have agreed to sleep at my home after the dance? Sleep right down the hall from my bedroom? She in her pajamas and I in my shorts—just a breath away from naked. We could have real sex. But I needed to buy condoms and I knew this would be difficult because I was cowardly about such things. I didn't think I could just walk into a pharmacy and ask for condoms. Back then, they weren't out on a metal rack as they are today. Usually the pharmacist kept them hidden behind the counter and you had to ask for them. Asking was a dead giveaway.

The day of the dance I was in New York City painting my youngest older sister's apartment, which was on Waverly Place in Greenwich Village. There was no telephone in her apartment. I walked six blocks to a pay phone on the corner of Greenwich and 11th to call Lori Ann. I wanted to know what time she would be dropped off at Bruce's house, where my dad and I would pick her up. I wanted to hear her voice—tell her how much I loved her. But the Quinn phone was busy.

On my second trip to the payphone I passed a pharmacy and knew what had to be done—I needed condoms—dozens of them because we were horny, Lori Ann and I. I needed to ask the pharmacist who was behind another counter blending ointments and liquids and powders with a spatula. He looked up. We made eye-contact.

"If you need something my assistant can help," he gestured toward a woman with gray hair and thick glasses who was sitting by the cash register and within reach of the condom rack.

"No, I need to speak with you," I said and I tried to get the wobble out of my voice.

"Are you old enough to buy condoms?" he said.

"I'm eighteen," I replied.

He smiled. "Okay, what kind do you prefer?"

"The safest ones you have." My voice cracked.

He smiled again. "Trojans are very good and the thicker ones will keep you stiff longer. It's better for your partner if you can stay erect longer." He was speaking softly, leaning over the counter so I could hear his advice.

I felt my face get hot. He was on to me—a first-timer—but I noted the advice.

"How many?" he asked.

I hesitated. "How much are they?"

"Fifty Cents apiece."

I handed him six dollars.

"Wow," he said. He put a dozen in a bag and I nodded my head in thanks and headed for the door just short of running. I heard them laughing before the door swung closed.

I tried Lori Ann's number six more times over four hours, walking each time from my sister's apartment to the payphone booth. The phone remained busy. Around 2pm, I called Bruce.

As soon as he recognized my voice he said, "Where have you been?"

I told him about my sister's apartment and the busy signal on the Quinn phone. I told him how excited I was about the upcoming evening.

"The phone isn't busy," he said. "Uncle Phil had it disconnected because he couldn't get through to his own house. The girls were gabbing all morning and he got pissed. He also grounded them. Sorry, friend," Bruce said, "No dance this weekend unless you want to take me."

"Ah fuck," I said. "This is awful."

"Really? Were you going to violate my cousin?"

"Come on Bruce. This isn't funny." And it wasn't. It was a life changing event for me.

After that day, Lori Ann slowly slipped away from me. I think someone else beat me into her pussy. I say this because in the Fall of that same year we went to an overlook on the Palisades Interstate Parkway where we could neck in the car. It was called going to the submarine races because this parking area overlooked the Hudson River near Storm King Mountain and why else would young couples park in such a place. Certainly not to explore external sex organs and so forth.

"Come on, do it," she whispered into my ear. Her tongue began to explore my ear. Her hand reached for my stiff dick. She had never done that before. I wanted to do it, but I kept thinking of the couple in the front seat—Lori Ann's best friend and her boyfriend. I kept thinking of Lori Ann's reputation. I mean, it was fine to fondle and have sex safely and in private, but not where someone else would know.

As these thoughts banged around inside of my head, Lori Ann began to tickle me, which ruined the atmosphere. I hated being tickled and was thrashing around in the back seat. Then the guy in the front seat apparently got his dick caught in his zipper which ended the evening on a sour note.

A week or two after the submarine race debacle, I accompanied Lori Ann to a dance at her high school. We were slow dancing to *Eddie My Love* when Lori Ann stepped back and flashed an odd expression at me. It reminded me of the expression my little nephew had when he was about to pass gas. She said, Michael, would you go wait for me in the parking lot.

"The parking lot?" I said. It was cold and windy outside.

"Please, Michael," she said. "I'll be out in a moment."

Lori Ann appeared in about ten minutes. Said she was confused and needed time to figure things out. It seemed sincere and I loved her so much I'd do anything for Lori Ann, so I said, "Sure," and left that dance. But all the way home on the bus there was a bad feeling about our future together.

A letter arrived a few days later. She had figured it out. It was a guy named O'Reilly. He was a year or two older and probably had already had sex with Lori Ann. She had cheered for him several times at a football game I attended to watch her cheer. She said she couldn't wait for me to finish my education, whether it was flying or doctoring or whatever. She said she needed to settle down and have a family as soon as she graduated high school.

Phillip Quinn changed the course of my life—mine and Lori Ann's—maybe others. That's how I've looked at that lost weekend opportunity in the spring of '56. Back then common wisdom for an Irish Catholic girl said the first guy into her vagina won ownership. Had she come to that Spring Dance, it might have been me. I might have made wild passionate love to her (even though I had no idea how to make wild passionate love) and she would have been my girl, forever.

It is probably reasonable to point out that any grasp I might have had on religion was lost as a result of the departure of Lori Ann Quinn from my life. Dealing with this calamity produced many hours of introspection and deconstruction of what I knew as reality at the time. Religion and god seemed nothing more than another perspective of the magic of lights far off on the horizon when I was very young at the beach. Religion was magic with a rule book and it ruined everything. An afterlife, something more than all the unimaginable possibilities—this was unnecessary for me. Lori Ann was very religious in an Irish Catholic kind of way and we probably would not have worked for this reason.

Still, I keep looking for another Guinevere. I have not found her. But sport-fucking found me. Some girls like sex as much as I do. They love their orgasms and any reasonably clean guy who can make that happen for them. I became quite good at this. But then, I met Mary Elizabeth O'Rourke and my mother's first poisoning occurred.

A FAMILY'S POWER

A FAMILY'S POWER

Parents and siblings factor into who you are—who you become. Sometimes they do so like a seemingly inert ingredient. My mother lived an unusual life. As a child her family enjoyed extraordinary wealth and privilege. Her mother descended from Murano Jews, her father was an Italian Jew who neither admitted to nor practiced his Judaic connection. The story I am aware of is that they ran off together to North Africa in 1900—never married because my grandmother was already married—or so she thought.

Her husband had gone to America and disappeared. She never heard of him or from him again. My grandfather was a civil engineer. He worked for a mining company in Tunis. Phosphates, iron, gold—I don't know but his family had great wealth. The original family patriarch was a Baron with lands and title given to him by a grateful Italian king who benefited from the financial support of my grandfather's family when Italy was finally unified under one monarch. The land given was mostly in Sicily and carried the family name.

My grandmother and grandfather had children together, three girls, Joyce, Ellenora, and Serina. Grandfather accumulated more wealth in North Africa and then, in 1909 or 1910, came to the United States. Mother, the middle daughter, was five. They didn't come in steerage or stop at Ellis Island. They came first class, brought an Arab manservant, and an Arabian gelding, black as night. The horse looked extraordinary in the old sepia photos with a muscular neck and a beautiful face and mane. And they brought furniture and clothing, rugs and silver, china and jewelry. They brought a carriage which that black Arabian pulled and the manservant in his finest turban and robe drove mother and her family in the carriage to the Metropolitan Opera House, during the season, for Saturday matinees. Mother would smile when she recalled those afternoons. And there was another sepia picture to document her memory, the black Arabian, the carriage, the Arab manservant holding the bridle—the opera house as background—mother waving from the carriage door.

Mother's parents owned a brownstone in Brooklyn, restaurant on the first floor, an apartment above. Most of the time, they lived in the apartment. But there was also my grandfather's farm somewhere out on Long Island and when they were there, the Arabian could run free in open pastures. The farm was out in what is now called the Hamptons.

Mother was to become a lawyer. Her father promised. She did not know, however, that her parents had no marriage certificate. She did not know Grandmother was ravaged by guilt because her first husband disappeared. Mother's half-sister by that first husband was Josephine who stayed in North Africa with my grandfather's brother, Tishian, when mother and her other sisters and parents came to America. Years later Josephine said her father was dead, so mother believed he was, but the truth will never be known.

Mother and Josephine wrote letters for years. Josephine eventually settled in Rome and taught grade school. Mother read the letters to me when I was a child—letters from Aunt Josephine in Rome. There was a picture. Josephine was misshapen—hunchbacked. Rickets as a child is what mother said.

But mother never mentioned the mess between her parents. Never offered details about the breakup of her family, about why another woman with a child my grandfather fathered got all of his money, the restaurant, the Brooklyn apartment, the Long Island farm. She said a judge ruled on the matter and she never understood. Thought it might have been because grandmother was acting crazy in those days, consulting fortune tellers, pissing away what little money she had to find out about her first husband from soothsayers.

Years later, at my mother's funeral an old man kept staring at me. I did not recognize him. I walked across the room and confronted him.

"Why are you staring at me?"

"You look like your grandfather."

"Which one?" I asked.

"Your mother's father," he said with a kind smile.

The old man was my grandfather's cousin. He told me the story as he knew it and this is how I came to know it. He said my grandfather was a powerful man with a great deal of money. I wondered where it all had gone.

"They never married," he said. "In those days they were courageous intellectuals. Ran off to North Africa and lived together—had children together."

This was apparently why Josephine did not go with them to America. And why the judge had no choice. Grandfather had a lawful young wife and it wasn't grandmother. Still, wouldn't a judge have considered three young children? Mother was 11 when her father died. Serina was 9 and Joyce 13. Perhaps bastard children and grandchildren had no status back then.

Mother said Grandmother drove Grandfather to his death, crazy with guilt over her first husband. According to Mother, Grandmother was not a good loving wife. And by loving I wondered if mother was talking about sex. Nonetheless she ran off with him and had three children with him. But mother didn't know most of that story, or if she did, she never shared or admitted it. Had my grandfather married another woman because of my grandmother's sex issues, or perhaps mental illness issues? Why had he said nothing of this? Did he hate my grandmother?

After she had oldest older sister, my mother said she did not want more children with my father. Mother was not a happy person. Mother, like her parents was an intellectual. My father was not. He was a simple earthy man. He liked women, cards, detective stories, prize fighting. Anthony Quinn would play my father in a movie. Mother fell for him. He wrote my mother poetry. Later she discovered he copied it from magazines. Then she wanted out because life was difficult with my father, and Mother had had enough of life's difficulties. And there was another man who loved her. His name was Jack. Wanted to take her to California with him but she wouldn't or couldn't do it for reasons known only to her. My mother's face often spoke of regrets.

So, she learned to empty her own uterus. She told me about it. Used Epsom Salts; dilated and curettaged herself with an instrument she constructed from an old wire coat hanger—knew to boil it in water first. In this way many of my would-be siblings were scraped and flushed from existence. Youngest older sister survived the curette and I survived, born in 1940 when FDR was President, Steinbeck's *The Grapes of Wrath* won the Pulitzer and no Nobel Peace Prize was awarded.

At five I stopped speaking to my mother for six months. The silence began when she hemorrhaged and fell to the floor—begged me to help her. Said I must call for help and pointed to the telephone. I lifted the receiver—heavy black metal. A voice asked a question about numbers.

I said something like, "Mommy is on the floor in blood."

"Where do you live?"

"120 Oak Street." I'd been taught my address in case I got lost.

Police and an ambulance arrived and Mother disappeared out the door. The police took me to their station—left a note for my dad in the house.

Mother was gone a long while. My sisters and grandmother took care of me. I did not miss my mother because I didn't miss people who pulled out hair, bled and fell to the floor. When she returned I would not speak to her. "She's not my mommy," is what I said at the time.

It was a nervous breakdown. It was cervical cancer. Mother recovered. She was patient with me—kind and funny. One day after about six months had passed she made me laugh because she sat one of my toy soldiers on a toy toilet that my uncle Bob had made and she did pooping sounds with her mouth. In this way she became my mother again. But something happened to me back then. I began to learn how to remove guilt from my feelings and that I could only count on myself.

When I was ten, she started to slip, again. Began to hate Dad, again. Screamed at him and pulled at her hair, again. He broke furniture and shouted back at her, again. Home was not a good place—again. But I had a shelter within myself where I could hide. It was a quiet place—a place where I felt strong and in charge. I was a warrior knight. I needed no one.

I went to Mendham with my oldest older sister whenever I could. She was renting the upper floor of a farmhouse while her husband was in Korea fighting a war. In Mendham I talked to goats and tadpoles. I grew courage by not sidestepping a charging ram. If timed just right you could grab the horns like handlebars and ride forward on the goats head. There was also electrified fence on that farm. I could hold on for almost a minute before I had to let go. This was another test I devised to build my courage and resolve so I needed no one.

With older sister I did not have to deal with mother saying no to everything I wanted—any toy or even an article of clothing. If I said I wanted it Mother said I'd be stronger if I did without it.

"I could have left all of this, years ago, and gone off with a man who really loved me," mother said as she fed the washed clothing into the ringer which I was cranking.

"Why didn't you?" I asked.

"I loved my children too much to leave."

"Wasn't that before Connie and I were born?"

She didn't answer. Took the laundry outside and hung it on the cloths line.

I liked to look at her pencil sketches when I was in the basement. She kept her portfolio under the stairs and said yes if I asked to see it. She did the work while she was in college at Cooper Union studying clothing design.

"Want to keep me company while I mend some shirts?" she said when she got back from hanging laundry.

"Okay," I said even though I'd rather have gone outside and rode my bike.

We climbed the steps to the second floor of the old house. The second floor smelled of Grandma's burned orange peels. She burned them on her small electric hot plate to hide other smells like cooked bacon or garlic.

As mother began to sew she said, "Your father and I have wonderful sex together."

She said, "Your father had sex with Aunt Joyce and it was a terrible thing. I almost lost my mind." As she spoke she did not take her eyes off the garment she was pushing past the needle that rapidly rose and fell, but her voice was steady and flat.

At ten I knew something of sex, small veiled mysteries, but I didn't know why mother told me this and I was too naïve to become embarrassed. She had to pedal by rocking her foot back and forth on an ornate black metal grate the size of a magazine cover to make the needle rise and fall. I was looking out the second floor window of Mother's small sewing room. I was looking at cherry blossoms and imagining how delicious the cherries would be if the birds didn't get to them first. I wanted to climb the tree and pick cherries as soon as they appeared.

But I was confused about Dad and Aunt Joyce. Do husbands customarily have sex with their wife's sister? Later, I checked with my oldest older sister who confirmed the story. She said, "I had to go get Daddy from Aunt Joyce's. But you're too young to know about that. Did Mom actually tell you that?"

"Did you see them having sex?" I asked, not sure of what having sex looked like but suspecting it might have been something like having a bath with my former babysitter.

"No." And oldest older sister seemed annoyed.

"Then how do you know they did it?"

Sissy didn't answer (I called my oldest older sister, Sissy).

It was hard to believe that my dad would have had sex with Aunt Joyce because Aunt Joyce was fat and whenever I visited her house she smelled bad—like my underwear when I farted and passed more than gas. I didn't think Aunt Joyce could actually wipe her ass after she pooped because she was so fat and her arms seemed too short. And besides, if sex is such a great and desirable thing, why would my dad want it with Aunt Joyce? I thought of that babysitter who was not fat and smelled of flowers. I wondered if at the time we may have been playing at something that had to do with sex.

Mother got stronger and easier to be with when she began to work with the mentally ill. It may have had something to do with my youngest older sister, Gloria, who changed her name to Connie. Connie had a drug problem and an alcohol problem and her mood swings were fast and scary. I think Mother felt responsible for Connie's problems—like she hadn't been a good mother because of her issues, the ones that led to that nervous breakdown. So Mother volunteered her time. She established a halfway house. She was an advocate. Mother, like the rest of us, was flawed, but she knew it and tried to grow. Mother was a psychologically oriented person. She read psychology books and philosophy books and talked and figured lots of things out. I think she taught me to deconstruct mysteries.

Surviving the on and off again Felini movie scenes at our house made me strong. Mother deconstructed everything, it seemed. She asked me what I wanted to be when I grew up.

"A fighter pilot," I said.

"Pilots are bums. They die in crashes or wars. Cannon fodder," she said. "You should become a lawyer or a doctor or an architect," she said. "You could learn music. That's good for you, too."

There was plenty of musical talent in the family. One aunt could sing opera. My dad played piano and had never had a lesson. Connie was offered a scholarship to Julliard.

"I want to be an astronomer," I said.

"They don't make much money," she said.

"I love pretty women, not money," I said.

She said, "If you're not careful you'll be just like your father."

She never said I might be like Connie or like her. What was so bad about my father?

"The un-irritated oyster creates no pearl," she said for the umpteenth time.

While in high school, one of my teachers asked me where I came from. "My mother's uterus," I replied after a moments thought. The teacher sent me to the principal's office. I told the principal the answer was accurate. The principal told me to stop being a smart-ass. "You get good grades," he said. "You're the smartest one in your family. It's time you grow up."

In a small town the principal can know if you are the smartest one in your family. Actually I think Connie was the smartest of my parents' children, but she was badly damaged. Mother said she and Dad were responsible for that damage.

"She was always having asthma attacks and I worried she was going to die." That's what Mother said. I wondered why she didn't feel any motherly concern about the ones she hooked and flushed. Maybe she did or maybe she thought no existence was better than a fucked-up existence. Mother knew a lot. She said we'd win the war and we did. She said Billy Connelly would probably commit suicide like his father and Billy hanged himself when he was sixteen. Mother said Truman would be a good president. He'd finish what Roosevelt started. She said Connie would have a sad life.

In 1944 when one of our cousins came home from France in a flag-draped coffin Mother cried. Cousin Thomas was a tail-gunner in a B17. The coffin was closed at the wake. Mother said he wasn't fit to be seen—all chewed up by bullets and then the fire from the crash. I wanted to know how anyone knew for sure it was Cousin Thomas if they didn't look. Mother pinched my ear. It was her way of telling me some things are better left unsaid.

Years later, she said I shouldn't go to the Air Force Academy and I didn't like that idea but I followed her suggestion. I didn't like her repeatedly implying my father wasn't a good provider or a steady partner but I didn't say so to her because some things are better left unsaid. Dad put up with her nervous breakdowns. He was there for me. He never left her. That's what I thought. And she always put Connie down, predicting bad things that all actually happened.

Perhaps it was being my mother's shrink that eventually convinced me to become a warrior—the knight I dreamed of being. Warriors are inserted and extracted, they have a mission.

Still, Mother believed it was a good thing, becoming a physician or a lawyer. I thought I might do more good as a knight. But Mother was more powerful than I suspected. I think her power over me pissed me off.

L

Dad was consistent. He wanted a son. When my sister Connie was a baby he used to pull down her pants and tell everyone to look at the penis. She's really a boy, he'd say. He did that to Connie. I don't think it was a good thing to do.

According to the history of my father's family name, Dad was the grandson of a farmer who came from Alsace Lorraine in the early years of the Civil War. This immigrant farmer settled in Ohio and got his citizenship by joining the Union Army. His son, my father's father, fought in the Spanish-American War then settled in Pennsylvania.

My father wanted to fight in a war. He enlisted in the army during WW I. He was only 16 but lied about his age. The story he told was that he ate a huge bunch of bananas so he would make the necessary weight for induction. It worked and he got into the Philadelphia Transport Command, Headquarters Company. That's what it says on the picture I have where he looks very small and very young. Dad told me the day the unit was boarding ship for France he got sick and was sent to the hospital. He had Typhoid Fever. Never went to France. But his unit did and Headquarters Company got gassed with chlorine. Many died. The rest were invalids for life.

Dad was lucky but he didn't think so. A few years after he didn't go to war and after the Typhoid Fever was cured, there was an accident. He drove a delivery truck. Every morning he stopped at a store for coffee and a buttered hard role. He would park the truck and go inside. There was a little kid who admired my father. Always wanted to ride with him or crank the truck to start the engine. I guess the kid thought he was doing my dad a favor the morning he tried to crank the truck when my dad was in the store. Dad left it in gear and when the kid cranked, the engine came to life and smashed the kid's head against the wall the truck was facing. My father felt he killed that boy because the truck was in gear.

He told that story until he couldn't tell stories anymore. I'd always remind him that it was normal to leave a truck in gear so it wouldn't roll. He'd shake his head in agreement but the look on his face was sad and responsible. I think that kid's death defined my father as a fearful man because all his boyhood friends said he was full of wildness and fearless before that happened. When he was my father he was fearful of many things. Not in a cowardly way, he'd stand up to anyone who threatened his family.

After the war he was a prizefighter—bantam weight. He knew how to box, bob and weave, throw the old one-two punch. Those same friends told me my father was a good boxer. But when his cousin Sal, the heavy weight, ran into Max Baer and got his brains punched out, my father's mother begged him to stop boxing. And when the truck killed the kid, my father lost interest in wildness and fearlessness. He became slow-moving and simple in his desires. When he met my mother he thought she was something. He was 24 and she was 19. He called her "Kid."

But Mother overpowered my father and didn't much admire him. He only had an eighth grade education. He did speak two languages, Italian and English. His mother was Italian-born so he spoke Italian. His father spoke English and Italian. I don't know if Grandfather spoke any German or French but my great grandfather who came from Alsace spoke German. I think my father's generation and the ones who came before were just glad to have a life. There seemed little concern for family history. The little I learned was from the letters of a grand-aunt of my father's from Ohio. Mostly they lived in the present. Dad never spoke of his grandfather. I hardly remember my father's parents except that his mother was very old and blind and died when I was four or five. Grandpa was also very old when I knew him—hunched over, bald, and demented. I remember him mostly in a bed at the VA hospital in Philadelphia. We visited for years. He always smiled when he saw us and when he died, my dad looked sad.

Like my father, my grandfather suffered from strokes and dementia. Nonetheless Grandfather lived into his nineties recognizing little of himself or his family. My dad lived until he was almost eighty but he also didn't know anyone or anything for several years before he died.

When he first got sick at seventy, I was in Vietnam. He recovered from that first stroke. It was a problem with his heart rhythm that started the ruination of his brain. Atrial fibrillation. The heart beats fast and irregularly and blood can't get out fast enough so it starts to clot from sitting and then those clots are fired out to the brain where brain cells die and a father who worked hard and loved you without condition turns into something closer to a tree or a carrot. My dad lost all of his dignity because of his illness. My mother allowed it to happen—the loss of dignity. She abandoned him in that fucking VA hospital.

"You don't understand how hard it is for me," she said.

"Fuck you," I thought, because she had promised for better or for worse, but she dumped him when it got worse and he'd shit himself and piss on himself and cry when the orderlies took him to the shower and hosed him off like an animal. More human bullshit—for better or for worse—maybe no one can make that kind of a deal.

Dad didn't love with conditions like my mother did. She would turn on me if I deviated from her expectations of son-ship, which I did on numerous occasions. Dad loved you no matter what. Like the night I pinned him against the wall in the kitchen because he wouldn't let me have the car to visit some girlfriend I was fucking. He didn't get angry with me. He just cried. I felt like a shit. I apologized sincerely and repeatedly and I hope he forgave me.

The first time he had one of the bad strokes that began to steal away his mind I sat with him and told him what a great dad he had been. I thanked him for his unconditional love. I think he understood because there were tears streaming down his cheeks as I spoke to him, held his hand and kissed him on the forehead. I was lucky for that opportunity. Dad died shortly after, in that VA hospital. I was out of the country at the time. I had become a warrior.

My oldest older sister had to handle things. "Sissy" turned into "Sister" sometime while I was in high school. We were always close. She seemed able to restrain at least some of Mother and Dad's bad behavior. She went off to nursing school in 1943, leaving me with a mother in terrible emotional distress and a father who didn't seem to notice. Although she left home, she visited often and introduced me to her classmates. She babied me, spoiled me, and overly indulged me. She and my father were the major reason for my very healthy ego and sense of worth and approval. I developed extraordinary self-esteem and confidence because of the manner of their love for me. I was lucky to have them—even Mother, despite her poison.

Sister was miss congeniality—the girl next door. She attracted the more conventional young man, one of whom, Joe Newmann, was a high school classmate who enlisted in the US Army right after graduation and fought in Germany during WWII. He was shot and decorated. Joe had asked Sister to write to him and that's how it got started. They married in 1947. But before Joe, there were entire teams of young boys at our home.

Sister was a cheerleader in high school. The basketball team loved her. Athletes loved her. Joe was a gymnast. He was born in Germany and came to the US as a very young boy. He loved his gymnastics. But Joe was shy and quiet, unlike most of the other boys who called on Sister. And Mother really liked him because he seemed disciplined and sensible.

My oldest older sister wanted to be a physician. Apparently Mother made it quite clear to her that girls married and raised families. "If you want to be in medicine, be a nurse," mother had said.

And there was a young doctor who had touched my sister's heart. But that was after she married Joe—after WWII while he was in Uppsala College and she was working at a hospital in New York City. The young physician was Canadian. He loved her—asked her to run away to Canada with him. But she couldn't or didn't. She stayed with Joe. They raised three boys. One belonged to youngest older sister who was in no condition to raise him because of the booze and pills.

I don't know if they're happy or despairing. My oldest older sister does not talk about unpleasant things. I'm not sure she even admits to herself that they exist. It was difficult for her, handling Dad's death. I think there may have been a mixture of guilt and sorrow with a splash of anger. Why didn't she rate medical school?

But here is the key—the males in my family all served in the military. From the Civil War to the Spanish American War, from World War I to Korea, there were Ross family men and a son-in-law in uniform. My turn would come to serve. I was eagerly waiting.

MARY ELIZABETH O'ROURKE

MARY ELIZABETH O'ROURKE

You have seen something of my life before she came into it. It wasn't complicated, really, and it was going along reasonably well until my roommate and good friend, Leo McDougal, set up a blind date for me in junior year of college. McDougal, whom I called Lee, said she was my kind of girl—funny, smart, good looking, penny loafers. She was a friend of his girl, who also went to Swarthmore. But on that blind date this girl and I traded insults for the entire evening. At one point I asked her to reach into the glove box and hand me my cigarettes. Driving did not allow me to safely do it myself. She said, "What am I, your slave? Get it yourself." During the movie, she made numerous comments about the shortcomings in plot and characterization—her criticism so constantly interrupting that keeping track of the story and action was impossible. After the movie, which was at a theater in Fort Lee, New Jersey, and therefore much less expensive than a New York City theater, I suggested we go to a diner in Fort Lee for sandwiches and coffee. The place was well known for its good food and generous helpings. She said she didn't eat at greasy-spoon diners. Also seemed irritated that we had not gone to a movie on Times Square. She and Lee's girl friend had taken a train from Philadelphia to Penn Station. They were expecting an evening out in New York City. I didn't have that kind of money.

So I drove them back to their hotel. My mind was on escaping this spoiled self-centered bitch. Nonetheless, I escorted her to the elevator in her upscale hotel with the gold doors, crystal knobs, and marble lobby décor. It was an act of duty because I never wanted to see her again.

"You're a little rich bitch," I said.

She laughed. "Maybe, but guys keep coming back for more," she said. Her tone was more uncomfortable than arrogant and accompanied by a nervous chortle.

Fuck you, was what I thought as I walked away, but I didn't say it. Lee wasn't far behind. He and his girl, Melody, were necking in the car and the hotel door man got pissed. I apologized to the doorman and Lee came running out of the lobby and hopped into the shotgun seat.

"I'm sorry about that," he said. "I didn't know she could be such a bitch."

Lovey Cohen was my girl when I met Mary Elizabeth. Lovey was one of those adorable young women. Years later when I first saw Charlize Theron in a movie I thought she might be Lovey's daughter. Then I heard Theron was born in South Africa—probably not Lovey's daughter. Yes, Lovey was a looker, made great grades in school and could hold a conversation about almost anything. She was shy, but cute like Lori Ann and she enjoyed sex-play. She even enjoyed food at the Parkside Diner up in Fort Lee. She was perfect for me but I didn't recognize it at the time. There was a problem—she was Jewish and I wasn't. At least that's what I thought back then because Mother was with-holding information. Nonetheless, I really thought Lovey might be the one, but for the Jewish thing, which was a serious issue in the 1950's and early sixties.

In those years religious tolerance was not the ideal. You were supposed to marry your own kind, which for me pointed to a Catholic because although Mother denied any formal religious affiliation, she sent me to the local Catholic Church and to catechism classes—the Murano charade (Murano Jews were those Jews in Spain during the reign of Queen Isabella and the Spanish Inquisition who alleged to give up their Jewishness in order to not be burned alive or forced out of Spain in a hurry) was still at work in my family centuries later. Nonetheless, by the time I dated Lovey Cohen I was well on the path toward atheism and someone's religious assignment meant nothing to me.

I had no idea how religious Lovey and her family were. In high school other Jewish girls wouldn't go out with me because I wasn't Jewish. Or if they did go out with me it was clear that the relationship would not get serious. Her company was wonderful, but I figured Lovey was not a long term possibility. I loved our sex-play. It was serious foreplay but the condom-thing was in my head as was cowardice or perhaps ambivalence regarding the whole respect-for-the-female issue so intercourse never happened between us, although I think it could have and I certainly wanted it to happen. Mostly, I didn't want to become seriously involved with Lovey and then get dumped again because I wasn't a Jew. So, my heart remained close.

Intercourse probably would have happened one night when Bruce kept calling wanting us to go with him and his date to the Central Plaza to listen and dance to Conrad Janis' Dixieland music and drink beer. My parents were out of town and Lovey and I were working on an evening of sex. She was affectionate and happy and very loving. But Bruce was persistent. I should have taken the phone off the hook.

The conflict about wanting to make love, falling in love, cherishing a lifelong relationship versus the ideal of being a gentleman—respecting a young woman's virginity until she was married—what a knight should do, wouldn't let me be. However, I'm not sure this conflict was recognizable at the time. I just saw myself as a coward.

And Lovey was a senior in high school. I was a college junior at Columbia. Now, I'd say so what. But back then it didn't feel right. I thought I might be taking advantage of her because I was so many years older.

I was headed to Lovey's house on that summer evening in '61 when fate and my mother's poison began to turn on me. I rang the doorbell and her mother opened the door. Mrs. Cohen said I needed to call home and there was an urgency in her tone.

"What happened," I said. "Is everything okay?" I was speaking softly to my mother into the wall phone in the Cohen's kitchen.

"Of course. Everything is fine," my mother said. "Call Mary Elizabeth O'Rourke as soon as possible. She called and wants you to join her family at the shore this weekend. She has to know tonight if you can come."

"For christ's sake, Mother, I'm on a date." I said. I figured Mary Elizabeth was in a big hurry because if I couldn't make it she needed time to ask someone else. Mary Elizabeth was definitely an absolute selfish bitch. Why did she want to pursue a relationship with me when I had made it so clear that I did not like her? My sisters always said I was handsome, and some girls had mentioned this to me, my dimples and that I resembled Rory Calhoun. But a rich girl like Mary Elizabeth could probably find plenty of handsome guys to date. She wasn't bad looking. She had an Irish face and an Irish smile. She was okay to look at and her body was nice.

"Watch your language!" my mother said.

"I'm alone in the kitchen," I said.

"Well then call Mary Elizabeth and tell her you can come."

"I hate that girl."

"You need to go. Trust your mother on this one."

"Well then you call her and tell her you'll go in my place." I said goodbye and placed the phone back in its wall cradle before Mother could add any words. Mary Elizabeth O'Rourke was history.

Later that night Lovey and I had a particularly passionate goodnight in the stairwell of her apartment building. If we were in a private place there could have been serious sex, again. After, as I walked down the stairs, I turned to look at her, to see that she had gotten into her door. But she was still on the top step looking down at me—a very sad face trying to smile. So very lovely to look at. What was wrong with me?

Mother called Mary Elizabeth and accepted the invitation for me. She said I was working and couldn't call back myself—apologized because I didn't call myself.

I was trapped. My little British sports car, the '54 MG ragtop, was too unreliable to take to the shore. It had too many mechanical problems and a leaky top. My parents didn't offer their car because they had plans. So I boarded a bus in New York City, got off one hundred miles and several hours later at a remote intersection in Manahauken where there was an old wooden *ESSO* station with chipped peeling white paint from the blowing sand that blasted that paint every hour of every day. Knurled scrub pines filled the view as far as the eye could see. The trip was a familiar one made many times before as a kid to spend a long summer weekend with my friend Ed and his folks at Ship Bottom during Junior High and High School. Same bus, the same station. Ed and his dad would pick me up and we'd talk about how great the fishing had been during the previous week as we drove from the station over the causeway out to the Island. I'd visit on the middle weekend of their vacation, Thursday till Sunday.

A black Lincoln sedan was parked at the *ESSO* station. A white-haired man and Mary Elizabeth stood beside the car. She was wearing green plaid Bermuda shorts, a pretty sleeveless white blouse and white canvas sneakers. The older guy had on suit trousers held up by black suspenders, the kind that button to the pants, a short sleeve dress shirt with the collar opened and black wingtips on his feet. The two of them were all smiles. I grabbed my canvas duffle from the overhead rack and exited the Trailways bus into the midday summer heat—a July Saturday at the Jersey Shore.

"Hi," Mary Elizabeth called and waved at me. Her smile wasn't quite a smile. It was tentative and shaky, the way her voice often sounded. Mary Elizabeth was nervous but always able to perform. She was pretentious. Her stepmother and aunts were responsible. Pretentious people have a problem with moment to moment discomfort because they're more concerned with what people are seeing and thinking about them than with just being themselves. This was another negative Mary Elizabeth feature.

"Michael Ross," right?" the gray-haired guy said. He was easy and pleasant. I liked him before I got to know him.

"Michael, this is my father, David O'Rourke," Mary Elizabeth said immediately accompanied by that chortle. It sounded like a hatchling jay calling for food.

"Sir," I said and shook his hand—firmly—the way I'd been taught.

Right from the start he treated me kindly and respectfully. We discussed the weather and ocean conditions. He offered me a smoke but I said I didn't smoke. We drove across the causeway where little seemed to have changed from summer days years back when Ed's dad picked me up and drove me from the bus station over the same causeway. The bay was choppy from the thousands of weekend boaters and fisherman. I inhaled the scent of bay air: salt, a hint of cauliflower, and yes, suntan lotion. It was a scent I had grown to love since my childhood because the ocean was one place where my family went to play and rest. The scent connected me with happy moments.

The O'Rourkes were in Beach Haven, several rungs up the ladder from Ship Bottom. The house was lovely. Just off the beach with a delightful balcony bathed in sea breeze. The bay added that cauliflower odor at low tide, but the beach smelled only of salt water and suntan lotion. I filled my lungs with that scent of peace and happiness. I had lifeguarded on Island Beach State Park the summer before. Sea water and suntan lotion reminded me of the many lovely young girls who liked hanging around with lifeguards. It was some kind of status symbol and afforded many wonderful opportunities to gain sexual experience. Being terminally shy, I had not learned much.

Margaret O'Rourke was what I had come to recognize as an Irish Catholic woman—very thin, brown hair, perfect nose but teeth in need of serious attention. She was pretentious. If you were attentive, you noticed her eyes following your moves. You noticed hesitations after she made a comment. She was measuring the effect. She wanted to be sure you saw her as she wanted to be seen. She wanted to be sure you were what she was looking for in the moment. Margaret O'Rourke was a busy little bee. She wanted to climb that social ladder—Mary Elizabeth's cousin's boyfriend who attended Brown University observed this fact when I met him that evening. He said, "Those Harrigan sisters are working hard to reach the top."

The Harrigan sisters included Mary Elizabeth's stepmother and three others. Margaret O'Rourke was pleasant and friendly. She insured that I felt welcome. She had raised Mary Elizabeth after her mother died giving birth to her and in everyway except the genetics, was Mary Elizabeth's mother.

Mary Elizabeth was nothing like she had been on our first date. Her father loaned me the Lincoln and we drove up to join one of Mary Elizabeth's classmates who summered in Spring Lake. Mary Elizabeth's cousin and her boyfriend from Brown also joined us at a roadhouse. I knew him because we played football against one another in the Ivy League. I was impressed by Mary Elizabeth's shore scene, so different from the one I knew—crowded sweatboxes, peeling paint, Salvation Army quality furnishings, cracked and bent cookware and dinnerware—hotels or cottages crowded together on sweltering streets, blocks from the beach. Mary Elizabeth's shore was more like the one I might have occasionally seen in movies or heard about from wealthy classmates who summered in the Hamptons. Something out of Gatsby's world.

The roadhouse, however, was the same—lots of beer and loud music along with enough cigarette smoke to choke on. Roadhouses were popular in the early 60s—up and coming bands, crowded dance floors and beverages including beer and booze. Mary Elizabeth, her cousin, her girlfriend and their dates all drank beer or booze. Mary Elizabeth liked rye whiskey and Seven-up or whiskey sours. I drank ginger ale. I bought into the idea that alcohol was poison to athletes, which I still saw myself as being. Mother said it was a poison to the human spirit and therefore very dangerous stuff. She pushed this agenda and I subscribed for years (although if the setting were relaxed and joyful mother could down a Manhattan or a whiskey sour and get silly). While in college, I drank ginger ale on the rocks whenever others drank booze or beer.

We had a good time. Laughed, danced, and discussed history, politics, music and literature and football. Mary Elizabeth was well educated and good with conversation. I looked at my surroundings, at what was going on and thought about Lovey and the stairwell. Lovey, so sweet and gentle and lovely to look at. Much more in line with my idea of what a girl should be like. But for reasons still unclear the idea of me in this other place that Mary Elizabeth inhabited was appealing.

I saw Lovey once more after that weekend with Mary Elizabeth. It was another passionate date. We spent it parked in my little British sports car. I slid the seats all the way back and lowered the seat

backs trying to get the shift lever out of play. If care was not taken
I worried it might wind up in someone's orifice and if anything was
going to be in an orifice it wasn't going to be the shift lever. Again,
I didn't have condoms so intercourse was out of the question. But
we both seemed to want intercourse. I apologized for not having
them and then for the wild, perhaps excessive passion. Lovey began to cry. I didn't understand her tears. In hindsight, perhaps
my perspective was on myself.

I held her and we started all over again. Control was
disappearing. I needed to leave before I did something I would live
to regret. Mother warned against the risks of unwanted untimely
pregnancy. How could I do such a thing to Lovey?

"You're an angel," I said. I wanted to tell her I loved her, but
I didn't. I wanted to kiss her and hold her face in my hands for
hours and hours, but I was feeling something dark and sinister.

"What's going to happen with us?" she asked.

"I don't know."

More tears.

"Look, you are the sweetest young woman I've ever know," I
said. And she was. I could so easily have committed to Lovey.
But I didn't say those words. I didn't say, "I love you and I want to
spend the rest of my life with you." I wanted to say them but they
wouldn't come out of my mouth.

A week later I went to Fort Devens, Massachusetts for ROTC summer training. When I returned it was Mary Elizabeth I dated. As

much as I missed Lovey and the passion of that relationship, there was something about Mary Elizabeth O'Rourke that held me. Her dad was very pleasant. During semester breaks, sometimes I'd go visit Mary Elizabeth in Roxbury. When I'd bring Mary Elizabeth home from a date at 1 or 2am, he'd make me steak and eggs.

Mary Elizabeth invited me to the 'mixers' at Swarthmore—an all female institution. Mixers are dances where young college girls invite young college guys from surrounding all male colleges or visa versa. We also frequented a roadhouse called "The Alibi." The relationship I shared with Mary Elizabeth O'Rourke was unusual. Beyond the timid French kissing at dates end, there was no passion. I wanted to explore sex-play with Mary Elizabeth as I had with Lori Ann, and Lovey, but Mary Elizabeth wouldn't allow it. "No, no, no," she'd say, "none of that for you." She was a good Catholic girl. She talked about sex and knew how to act sexy but there was no touching of private places. For me, this was going backwards instead of making healthy progress in sexual growth and development.

Mary Elizabeth was at her sexiest when she danced. She made moves. I kept waiting for her to relax and offer this passion to me off the dance floor. In my mind it was only a matter of time.

So Mary Elizabeth O'Rourke held my interest—the good conversation, the cute smile, my seemingly improved social status. She knew about opera and ballet. She had a wonderful sense of humor, dressed very well, and there was that nice body. Most of her cousins had gone to college. Her uncle was a physician. Mary Elizabeth usually said what was on her mind. Everything about Mary Elizabeth O'Rourke was great except the absence of passion in her heart. She never climbed all over me, kissed me like she wanted to go further. She never touched me except sometimes to put her arms around me when we kissed. When it came to passion and romance, Mary Elizabeth never acted like Lori Ann or Lovey. Never ever.

LEARNING THE TRADE

LEARNING THE TRADE

Jump school was jump school. Instructors screaming in your face, stories of disaster and heroics, running for miles every day, jumping off towers and finally the first static line jump. Jumping out of airplanes was not a pleasure for me. Getting my mind wired for that first step out the door, the ground so far below was my problem. One of my instructors may have seen it in my eyes. As I was about to go out the door of the C-119, he said, "Any day is a good day to die, Sir, but if you're Airborne it's less likely to be today."

As my chute filled with air there was a nerve-settling jerk upward as if the falling had been arrested. The instructor's words reverberated in my head as I slowly drifted toward the drop zone. It became clear to me that the more skilled I'd become, the less likely I'd waste my life with some meaningless death. A knight needed to live in order to serve well. The target field came up fast and I rolled perfectly, contained my parachute lines and pulled it in as instructed.

"Nice going Ross," one of the instructors called out as others in the jump tumbled out of control and tangled in their lines when they arrived on the ground.

"You may actually make it through this, Sir," the same instructor said with a smile, because during this training our rank was generally ignored.

ㄴ

In the summer and fall of '62, respectively, my Airborne training and Ranger training were completed. This training included mountain training in Georgia and Wyoming, desert training in Utah and swamp training in the Everglades. Then there was a week of leave at home. I had fucked numerous young Alabama and Georgia girls while away at Ranger School. Two cases of clap were the downside of the experience. The disgusting dripping and burning finally converted me to condom advocacy.

After discovering what it was like to fuck a young woman who wanted sex, the idea of Mary Elizabeth as a mate was even more ridiculous. She had to be unloaded. But despite my macho performance as an Airborne Ranger, in many social ways with females, I remained somewhat cowardly. The girls I had fucked were generally half in the bag and horny. They wanted to be fucked. It was necessary to simply provide the erect cock. Perhaps these coeds from various area colleges thought it an accomplishment to be fucked by a crew cut topped athletic muscular military officer. One of the girls who gave me gonorrhea definitely fucked me. She danced on my dick and was so wild and noisy I couldn't come until I turned her over and finished her on my own terms. Nonetheless, what I liked about sex and females became crystal clear and Mary Elizabeth had nothing to offer.

While on leave there was no desire to see her. My training had lasted almost five months. Leave would take me through Thanksgiving, but four days after, I had to report for duty at an Air

Force base in the Florida panhandle. It was the home of a special warfare unit which was to be my first duty station. At the end of those five months a promotion for meritorious performance to first lieutenant infantry was given to me. My next duty station held the promise of great adventures.

While at home, I visited with some old friends and caught up on local goings-on. One of my old girlfriends, Melissa, was married. A great sense of loss and sadness covered me when Mother told me about Melissa. Heidi, another former girlfriend agreed to a date. She had been and remained terribly shy. I wanted to make out with her and she said it was too soon to do that because we had not seen one another in years. Heidi was a nurse. I don't know just what I expected, but she didn't deliver so that was that. I wanted to see Lovey, but she was away on some college project. Mother arranged Mary Elizabeth's presence for Thanksgiving as a 'surprise.' Once again, my mother bush-wacked me. But Mary Elizabeth looked lovely. She knew how to be a class act. She was affectionate—even gave me an occasional peck on the cheek.

"I'm not going to medical school," I said to her while we were eating dinner.

"Well, you never know how fate can alter choices," she said and I left it at that. After dinner we reminisced about some fun times during college, and then I drove her to the train station. I tried to caress her pussy during a long wet kiss in the car, but she screamed at me. "Do you think I'm some kind of whore?"

"No, I'm just trying to give you some pleasure. I know for a fact that women can enjoy it."

"Well fuck you, buster," she said. "I don't."

"What are you, some kind of fucking lesbian?"

"Fuck you," she repeated and got out of my car, pulled her suitcase out of the back seat and walked toward the station entrance.

I rolled down the Monza window and spit the taste of her out of my mouth, lit a Lucky Strike and headed home.

Next day as I was packing my bag, Mother asked, "Did you enjoy your date with Mary Elizabeth?"

"I hate that bitch," I said. "Just quit trying to match me with her. No good can come of it."

After that brief conversation, I threw my bag in the front trunk, put the top down, hugged my mother and father and headed for the Florida Panhandle.

APPRENTICESHIP AND SOMETHING MORE

APPRENTICESHIP AND SOMETHING MORE

My billet at the air force base wasn't what I'd expected. I was imagining comfortable bachelor officer quarters. Instead five of us were in a dusty hot Quonset hut far off in an isolated section of the airbase. And we were not all members of the US Army. Two were US Navy, and one was a US Marine. What we had in common was that up until now we had had similar training. We knew how to jump from an airplane, and we knew how to survive and fight in various environments. We had all heard the words, 'elite fighting force' at some point. And we discovered in our initial conversation that we each had met and received a similar briefing while at college ROTC summer camp or Platoon Leader Class Marine Corps summer camp from the same Army Lt Colonel, Byron C. Taylor. We did not know why we were waiting by an isolated Quonset hut on the Florida panhandle airbase. Our orders said to report to Hurlburt Field. There was a notation stating that 'gate personnel' would direct us further upon arrival and the MPs at the Gate did just that.

"Sir, follow the main base road, to the circle, take the third right off the circle and follow that road until it turns to gravel. There'll be an old Quonset there with no identifying markings.

That is where you need to await further instructions, Sir. There will be someone there at 0600 hours." He then saluted smartly and I drove through the gate.

Each of us received the same instructions and now we stood inside the large Quonset. Inside the door was an office with a desk and chairs—five of them not including the chair behind the desk. There were five of us. There was another door beyond the desk that said PRIVATE in bold white letters about a foot from the top.

"What the hell kind of a deal is this," Mark said. He was navy, a Lt JG.

"Relax asshole," his fellow navel officer said. His name was Jim. Same rank.

"The orders say to report at 0600. It's 0556," the Marine said. His name was Josh. Like me and the other Army Airborne Ranger, Adam, Josh was a First Lieutenant. Our ranks were all equivalent except the Navy always had to be different. It was a Navy thing.

None of us had met before—never even seen one another that we could recall. At exactly 0600 hours by the clock on the wall behind the desk, the door opened and a very large first sergeant who filled the doorway as he passed through shouted, "Attention." A stocky bald Bird Colonel with a cigar clinched between his teeth walked into the room. He was my height, a little over six feet. He looked like a pro football linebacker and the sergeant looked like a nose guard.

"Relax gentlemen. Welcome to Special Warfare Command Center, Alpha team. That is who you are—Alpha team. This is First Sergeant Warren. He will be your house mother for the next few months. I'm your commander, Colonel Fritz Monfried. Everything that happens inside this building and during your training and after your training is top secret. You say nothing to anyone about what you do. You do not even use the designation

Alpha team. Only I and the First Sergeant use the designation Alpha team. You will continue to wear infantry designation brass or insignia on your uniform. You will otherwise wear no unit designation. You will avoid appearing in public in uniform unless specifically instructed to do so. On this base and during training you will wear only what you are given to wear. Is all of this clear to you?"

"Yes Sir," we responded in unison.

"Good. Sergeant Warren will now begin his job as your house mother." The colonel turned and left through the same door he had entered.

"I am not going to refer to any of you as 'Sir' except first thing in the morning and last thing in the evening. At those times I will address you properly and salute you as a team. You will all agree now to be known as Alpha Team collectively, and by your last name, otherwise. If you agree to this signify by saying I agree."

"I agree," we each repeated.

"Follow me Alpha Team."

We followed him out the front door and around to the back of the Quonset. There was another unmarked door like the one we had entered at the other end of the hut.

"Inside," he said.

We entered and noted the drab dark room with five cots and five standing lockers.

"Pick your bunk and get your personal stuff in here. Pull your cars around back and park them in the hangar across the yard."

He pointed out the open door to another smaller Quonset with no front or back.

"Drive them in and lock them. That will be your own private parking portico—because your officers."

He smiled with that wisecrack, but mostly to himself. He opened another door on the inside wall of what was to apparently be our quarters. There was another room with a pool table, a ping pong table, a card table, some comfortable easy chairs, a TV, and a record player.

"This is your home away from home, gentlemen. It has all the comforts of a love nest except I replace your love object. Unfortunately, I also will live in this building. Meals will be delivered to us when we are here."

He opened another door and there was another room resembling a kitchen with a refrigerator, table, sink, and plenty of counter space and cabinets.

"No maid service here," he said. "We clean up after ourselves. We will eat in here or in the field for the foreseeable future. Pay close attention and learn well," he said. "Soon you'll be working on your own and depending on one another."

The Quonset was our home for months but we traveled to many places from South America to the Middle East. It was on-the-job training. We jumped out of C-128s, and an upgraded B-26. We used a C-130B when we jumped from serious altitude and even made a few HALO jumps from a specially fitted U2. We were a go-anywhere-and- accomplish-the-mission team. Mostly, we performed 'surprise and destroy' missions. At the time, none of us knew where we actually fit into the military schematic. We had a CO, Colonel Fritz Monfried, a Regular Army type. We had a home base at Hurlbert Field. Any insignia on our uniform represented the unit to which we were attached at the time. It changed with different missions and sometimes we had no identifying insignias. Mostly when we were operational, we wore only our rank and US as subdued insignias sewn to the collars and lapels of black fatigues. We had dog tags with the usual information. We were Special Warfare Team Alpha, period.

Sergeant Warren appeared at all mission briefings and when we needed some special training on a new mission or a new weapon or some survival skill essential to a specific mission, but he did not accompany us on missions.

We had returned from South East Asia a week before—a special mission to remove a person of interest to the US Government. We worked with civilians in the highlands to accomplish our mission. We killed at least twelve VC on the mission. We killed them because they tried to discourage the mountain people with whom we were working from cooperating with us. To do this the VC took five infants from the tribe, slit their throats and hung them by their ankles from a tree. It was a statement to the Montagnard villagers.

Alpha Team also made a statement to the Montagnards. We hunted down and killed the VC baby-killers. It wasn't hard to find them because they were going from village to village bragging about what they had done and using there baby-killing as a threat to other villages if they even talked with us. We provided each one of the murdering bastards with a slow death assisted by the parents of those infants. We cut off cocks and lower legs and fingers. We removed tongues and noses. Then we used techniques developed by the English—we disemboweled them. I thoroughly enjoyed killing the murdering bastards. We pissed on their dead bodies and set their corpses on fire. We did it one by one and made the others watch and contemplate what they were about to experience. They screamed for mercy but we gave them none. Fuck them for killing babies.

The Montagnards learned that we were powerful friends. They were simple people who respected us for the simple justice we served on the VC—end of story.

So now we were sitting in the Quonset dayroom relaxing. We were due a leave. I had been writing to a few girls. I was hungry for pussy. I didn't just want some prostitute I could buy. I was thinking about Lovey. She should be in college somewhere. I planned on getting in touch with her mother. As this thought was coming together in my head, Colonel Fritz appeared at the door. Before we could jump to attention he said, "Relax, relax." He came in and sat in one of the easy chairs.

"Would you like a drink, Sir?" someone asked.

"Sure, a scotch and water if you have it. So how did the mission go? I know you brought back the individual we asked you to find and return, but I mean, how did it go, otherwise?"

I poured the drink and handed it to him. "The mission was a good one, Sir. We helped one Montagnard village meter out some justice to a group of VC who killed some of their babies."

"Yes, the word got back to some CIA people that one of the teams had cut up some VC and burned them. I'm sure that wasn't you people," he said. Then he added, "Any of you guys do well in College?"

It seemed like an innocuous enough question, especially camouflaged by the inquiry into our VC killing activities. "I did well, Sir," I said. No one else responded.

"Good, I want you to take the MCAT exam," he said.

I knew the MCAT exam was used to determine admittance to medical school. "Sir?" I said.

"We need docs in this command who are our own people— trained team members. Outsiders just can't make the grade."

MEDICAL SCHOOL

MEDICAL SCHOOL

I spent that leave taking a course to help me do well on the MCAT exam. I was to tell no one. The exam was a few months later and based on the results, Columbia P&S accepted me. I had been instructed to apply there. Turned out there was a fellow Army officer in my class. This was a good thing because most of the pre-meds at my college were difficult people. Phil Pizzani, like me, was Regular Army. He had attended VMI and was not like the pre-meds I had not liked at Columbia College. He was a smart, tough, pleasant and straightforward person. He was also with the teams, but not mine. Apparently, there were other teams and this was the first time I recognized this to be the case. Pizzani did not discuss his team nor did he ever ask me to discuss mine. But we knew that we were at Columbia P&S under the same military directive. Years later I discovered he was Delta Team.

Before news of my acceptance arrived, it was business as usual. We lived in the same old Quonset and missions continued. Some were assassination missions. Some were aimed at capturing known enemies to the US and delivering them to various places both in and out of the US. About one week before the first semester was to begin my acceptance and new orders arrived on the same day. The new orders placed me on indefinite leave to complete medical school and an internal medicine specialty. I went home to New

Jersey and shared the news with my parents. I found Lovey. She was a recent graduate of Barnard College and about to enter law school at Columbia University. However, she was engaged. Still, she agreed to meet me for dinner.

We met outside of Lafayette, a French restaurant I loved. We kissed and it was as it had been, or so I thought.

"Lovey, I love you. I want to marry you." The words flew out of my mouth.

She looked surprised. "I have to think about this, Michael. I think I love you, but I also love Harvey. You just disappeared. You never wrote or called."

We went inside and were seated at a quiet corner booth.

"I'm sorry. I was in training and serving in the military."

"You're in the military?"

It didn't sound like a good question. There was a tone in the way she said "military."

Her fiancé's name was Harvey. I didn't know him and didn't want to know him. I wanted Lovey to break the engagement. Harvey was Jewish and owned his own business. Perhaps this gave him an edge in Lovey's decision, although she said it didn't matter to her. Maybe it mattered to her parents. My future was career Army regardless of medical school. The war in South East Asia was heating up. At the time it wasn't popular and in many circles, neither was a military career.

"Please," I said. "I love you. Spend the rest of your life with me."

"I felt that way three years ago and then you disappeared," she said. "How do I know you won't disappear again?" She looked at me and there was that same look—the one she had had when I looked up the stairway at her years before.

There was no easy honest answer to that question because my military career might cause frequent disappearances. Maybe even a permanent disappearance. "I love you," I repeated. She smiled a warm loving smile but said nothing.

A week later I received a letter from Lovey. She was sticking with Harvey. I tried to call her but she would not take my calls. "Let her be, Michael," her mother said to me when she answered the phone on one of my attempts to reach Lovey at home. "It took her several years to get over you the last time you dropped out of her life. She seems happy with Harvey. If you really love her, let her be. Harvey will give her a good life."

Another girl I loved and another letter—enough was enough. My focus turned to scholarship. Because the first two summers of medical school included some time off, I taught infantry platoon level tactics at an Army infantry installation called Fort Dix.

Some months after that dinner date, Lovey called me and wanted to meet. We had two brief affairs before she married Harvey. We had sex—steamy exciting sex. But something made me feel relief when she went ahead and married Harvey. Then about a month after her wedding she called me and wanted to get together again.

"You're married now," I said. "I can't deal with that."

I don't understand what was up with my feelings because I still love her.

In early third year of medical school a promotion to Captain occurred. My MOS remained 81542—a foot soldier with special skills. The Army wasn't going to forget that fact. I had been trained to kill in many ways and not look back. My take on life was different than most people. I was not afraid of dying. Death was the natural end to life for everyone. How and when it occurred was a combination of chance, accident, choice, and something called synchronicity—a philosophical and mathematical concept of certain things happening together for reasons more quantum than measurable.

In third year, the clinical clerkships begin. Back then this was a time when the third year students actually began to treat ward patients—part of a team comprised of two third year students, two fourth year students, two interns and one first year resident. I was good with team play. There was a girl on my team, one of the interns. We fucked regularly when we had the time. On call rooms provided the perfect hideaway. My life at twenty-five was good but I missed the excitement of military missions, the adventure—night kills—ambushes.

A new perspective came together in my mind. As a physician/warrior, I could kill or I could heal. It was a choice—a good choice. Some people needed to be saved, and others eliminated. This perspective was reasonably simple for me to see most of the time. Like those VC who killed the Montagnard babies. They needed to be eliminated. The world was better without them. I knew this, the Montagnards knew this and my team members knew it. What kind of decent reasonable human beings kill babies—innocent little babies?

During the months when I was treating poor abandoned souls in what were then referred to as the boarder wards at Bellevue, the three-thousand bed receiving hospital for the entire city of New York, clear revelations appeared. These poor abandoned souls were burned-out alcoholics and heroin addicts from the streets of Manhattan. Mostly alcoholics. No one acknowledged any ties to these people. They lived in the hospital because they were sick in mind and body and there was no alternative for them. One of them, let's call him John, sat day and night in his bed or his bedside chair, and if a roll of toilet paper was within reach, he ate it. He would place the end of the roll in his mouth and slowly chew and draw in—chew and draw in, until the roll was gone. He also grabbed any nurse's ass he could. Mostly, the nurses thought it was funny. I thought it was pathetic—life coming to this. John only said one word, "Pussy," which he repeated when any female was nearby.

One day while making rounds with my team on the boarder ward for which we were responsible, we found John in a stupor. He was drooling and unresponsive. His abdomen was rock-hard. His temperature was 106 F. John was close to death. One of the interns, the one I was fucking, decided to call a surgical consult on John. A surgical resident came to see him and advised an exploratory laparotomy.

In those days, medical students and residents were responsible for medicating their patients. Each ward had a medication cabinet with most of the drugs needed to mix IVs and to treat daily recurring problems. Hospital pharmacies handled antibiotics and narcotics, but things like bicarbonate ampoules, vitamin C ampoules and potassium ampoules were in cabinets mostly left unlocked by charge nurses for the convenience of the doctors and themselves since the workloads where enormous and mostly the city hospitals were understaffed. Of course, at our hospital we also had nursing students who worked around the clock along with the medical students and house staff. We were one big happy fucking family.

Well it happened that an ampoule containing 40meq of potassium chloride was in my jacket pocket. It was supposed to go into a liter bottle of half normal saline on another of my patients, but I hadn't gotten to mix that IV as yet. There also was a fifty cc syringe in my pocket to draw up the potassium chloride and add it to the IV bottle so it would enter the patient slowly over 24 hours.

But here's the thing, potassium chloride if given rapidly into an IV line or a vein causes instant cardiac arrest. And since upon the death of body cells, huge quantities of potassium are released into the bodily fluids including the blood, it is not possible at autopsy to detect that a person has been killed by a bolus of 40meq of potassium chloride.

I knew this because I read whenever I could get to the library, which was frequently since I didn't need a lot of sleep. Potassium chloride as a means to euthanize poor suffering abandoned souls was well established. Since the ampoule and the syringe were in my pocket when John took a turn for his ending, my perspective was that some form of synchronicity was at work—something to do with meaningful chance. John needed help—protection from further suffering. It was no problem finding a moment at his bedside when no one noticed 40meq of potassium chloride being pushed into the IV line that was delivering the lactated Ringers solution the surgical intern had hung in preparation for taking John to the operating room.

When the nurse checked him a few minutes before the orderly was to arrive and help her transfer him to a gurney for his ride to the OR, she found John dead. The death certificate read "Acute Abdominal Crisis with Septic Shock—cause unknown," along with the dementia and numerous other diagnoses John had amassed in his several years as a boarder at the hospital.

I did something meaningful for John, advocated for him—gave him peace. Humans kill all the time. We kill in war. We kill in seeking justice. And here, I killed to give a tormented being some peace. And yes, we offer horses and dogs and cats among others, relief from suffering. So don't even consider giving me any shit about this. In so much of our alleged morality there is only a pathetic illusion of justice and ethics. We bullshit ourselves and others. Cause suffering and avoid responsibility in the name of doing what we call, 'right'. My intention was to remove bullshit and apply reason and logic across the board—to be a responsible human being. Go in peace old John.

THE DEVIL'S DANCE

THE DEVIL'S DANCE

I used some savings to put a down-payment on an apartment that went co-op on West 87th between Columbus and Central Park West. It was convenient for medical school and plenty of horny New York City females. One November weekend while relaxing in my favorite chair trying to decide what to do with a rare afternoon of free time, the doorbell buzzed and I walked to the handset used to answer on the wall by the apartment door. "Who's there?" I said into the receiver.

A female voice responded, "It's an old friend."

"Well, well, an old friend. Do I need to guess who, or should I just let you in and be surprised?"

"Let me in, and be surprised, Michael."

I knew the voice—Mary Elizabeth. How did she find me? Probably my mother at work again, trying to get me hooked-up with a young woman worthy of me. I was on the third floor in a walk-up and the footsteps coming up the last flight seemed almost ominous. I stepped into the hall and there was Mary Elizabeth. But, she really looked good. She knew how to look good. She offered a bright smile and when Mary Elizabeth smiled like that her eyes smiled, too. I liked what I saw. It was a Saturday and I had no plans. I was horny.

"I hope this is okay. Your mom told me where you were living. I'm still living in Roxbury with my folks, and teaching at Westchester State. I've missed you," she said. "Thought I'd take a chance you might be at home. I'm in New York City for the weekend to shop and visit the Cloisters Museum."

She surely had done just as she said, but somewhere in that little Irish-Catholic brain there was a plan at work and Mary Elizabeth knew exactly what it was and how to carry it through to completion. She was wearing a mini-skirt and a very provocative low-cut blouse. This package was all wrapped up in a fluffy gray fox coat. As she slipped off the coat her head turned slightly and delivered a coy smile. I was absorbing it all. Yes, I was horny.

"It is just fine," I said. "Especially if you're in the mood for a good fucking. You definitely look good enough to fuck—maybe even eat."

But here is the thing about Mary Elizabeth. She is clever, she is tough on the surface, and she is determined to get what she wants. Still, she has many nerve endings that are exposed, like a tooth with a deep cavity. As long as nothing enters the cavity, there is no sense of pain or discomfort. But a good dose of cold food, or a chew on something like a nut, and there is immediate and profound discomfort. I wanted to deliver this kind of experience to Mary Elizabeth. I despised her because I had her figured for a phony.

My prod was deep into her cavity and she was processing. She had her back turned to me. She slowly turned to face me and said, "So, Michael, I guess you are glad to see me." And there was that smile again. "But I can also tell you've been away from civilization for too long. I'll be happy to work on civilizing you."

I stepped toward her and took her into my arms. I kissed her and pressed myself into her body. She was soft and lacking in any substantial physical strength. She did not fight me. She returned the kiss and smiled when I opened my eyes and moved my head back to look at her.

"I have been here at Columbia P&S for almost three years," I said. "Hardly away from civilization, Dearie. The thing is I have been with females who enjoy sex. Have you had sex yet, Mary Elizabeth? Has anyone made love to you or fucked you? Have you longed for that?" I saw the tears begin to form, even felt some regret for the attack, but I was angry with this woman who seemed to need my life to carry her life and her dreams—this woman who was hiding something about her sexuality. I had never come across such a sexually repressed female.

She turned to pick up her coat from the chair where she had draped it. "You're a sick son-of-a-bitch Michael Ross. Fuck you."

"I'm ready whenever you are, Mary Elizabeth. Put your mouth where it will do some good."

"Why should I put up with this shit from you? Why should I?"

"You shouldn't unless you just can't resist me. Unless you are ready and willing to grow up and lose the mid-Victorian point-of-view and manner. I can't stand you in that mode. I want a woman who feels and loves with passion and is open to grow and change in positive ways. I don't want a fucking Irish Catholic virgin."

She stood perfectly still, tears now slowly running down each cheek. "I do love you," she said. "But I have some pride and self-respect. I won't be abused and cast off like dirty laundry."

"Fine, take off your cloths and let's have sex. There's no better way to get to know one another."

"I can't," she said.

"You're a fucking twenty-five year old virgin. What the fuck is wrong with you?"

"I'm not a virgin." She screamed it. "I was raped when I was 14 by some fucking smelly sick bastard." Now the tears were flowing and she was sobbing.

I took her in my arms but she pulled away with a violent twist. "I was a child, just walking to the bus stop in downtown Philly," she said, still sobbing so the words came out in staccato. "That filthy fucking bastard pulled me into an ally and fucked me. It happened so fast. And it hurt—it really hurt."

"What did you do?"

"Nothing. I walked the rest of the way to the bus stop and tried to forget it."

"You never told your parents or any friends?"

"What would the point have been? I'd still be just as fucked up."

"Maybe not. Maybe talking about it and working it through would have helped." Now I understood. I sat down but she didn't. "Come on, sit." I patted the worn leather sofa I had gotten from Good Will Industries. She remained standing and then walked to one of the two wing chairs that were part of the set. She sat. Then she stood again, still wearing the fur coat. Mary Elizabeth had been violated. Any wonder she hated sex.

"Come on. Take off the coat and sit. You blurted that out and told me for a reason Mary Elizabeth. You chose to tell me after years of keeping that a secret—your secret."

"I wish I hadn't. I wish I were dead." The sobbing began again.

"Dead eliminates any chance for anything. I know you probably believe in an afterlife…"

"I don't know what I believe, any more," she interrupted. She sat back in the leather wing chair.

"Come on, sit over here by me. I won't hurt you."

In all honesty, I wasn't sure the story was true. She might be capable of this kind of manipulation to get what she wanted. I didn't trust her. Still, she seemed vulnerable and helpless. Was she that good of an actress? A desire to protect her was taking form inside of me.

She rose slowly and took the three steps to the sofa, turned and sat beside me. I couldn't help but notice her legs in that mini skirt. She had great legs. I knew if there was any hope of ever fucking her, she had a lot of healing to do and I wasn't sure I wanted this kind of a challenge or the implied risks.

She was shivering. I put another log into the wood stove— one of the reasons I had selected this apartment. Fireplaces and woodstoves, the direct warmth, the flickering glow, the smell of burning wood. The railroad clock on the wall struck four and the light from outside was rapidly dimming—November in New York City. I had the blinds opened and could see some bare tree limbs and brown grass in the Park. The last light of a November Saturday was fading to purple. The view of the Park was partial because my apartment was the second building in from the Central Park West corner of West 87th.

My focus shifted for a moment to that world outside. I reminded myself that there is no time, that perhaps I could help this lovely young woman become whole again. And something happened as that thought rolled around in my head. I turned toward her and gently kissed her forehead. I put my arms around her and we sat there until the only light in the room was a soft flickering from the log embers behind the grated door of the wood stove. A red-hot piece of wood made a loud pop. I watched the ember bounce around in the stove as if trying to escape.

We did not make much progress regarding her painful past, but still she visited regularly—usually on weekends when I was not on call at the hospital. Sometimes she would cook for me. Once she even stayed over after she'd had a few too many at the Alibi.

The Alibi dates resumed a few weeks after her first visit to my apartment.

"Did you enjoy our dates back in college when we'd go dancing to the Alibi?" she had asked me one Saturday afternoon when we met for lunch at a small café across from the Park on the corner of 76th. We were sitting by the window. I had a mouth full of pastrami on rye with Russian.

"I enjoyed watching you dance," I said after swallowing prematurely and missing out on more pleasure from the delicious sandwich.

"Want to watch some more?" she asked with a definite provocative tone.

We went that night. I had the weekend off and was all caught up on my reading. She was still a great dancer. We were not dancing to the romantic tune, *The Way You Look Tonight* because Mary Elizabeth was not big on slow dancing. For some reason my mind slipped back to slow dancing with Lovey. But then Mary Elizabeth said, "Come on Captain, you are a captain right? Let's get close and snuggly." She took my hand and dragged me onto the dance floor. She moved in tight and close. She was kissing me on the ear as we danced.

We hadn't had sex. We had kissed and even fallen asleep together on my sofa. But I was careful. Mary Elizabeth was a wounded animal. You had to be slow and cautious with wounded animals. She had had a few Seven-Up and rye whiskeys, a drink called a Seven and Seven.

"I love you, Michael," she said. "I don't want to lose you. I'll be okay, I promise."

I didn't say anything. I didn't know what to say. This was the former Miss Iceberg in my arms. I wanted great sex for as long as I could have sex. I didn't want some fucked up girl who couldn't get over a terribly traumatic experience in her past.

"Looks and charm and personality, I've got all of them and you've got me." I sang the words.

"No, I'm serious. Let me prove it to you."

We went back to my apartment and we made love. It wasn't great, but it was nice. It was sweet. I figured this was one hell of an accomplishment for Mary Elizabeth. Perhaps she really did love me.

A few weeks later, her stepmother was admitted to a small hospital over in Pennsylvania because of headaches and dizziness. The doctors over there couldn't make heads or tails out of her condition. I offered to speak to one of my professors to have her transferred to the Neurological Institute at Columbia, even suggested the University of Pennsylvania hospital in Philadelphia, but her family didn't want to do that. I think they felt it would be an insult to her stepmother's brother who was also her physician. He seemed a decent enough fellow, but he was a GP who had trained at a small local community hospital. The Neurological Institute at Columbia P&S was deservedly world famous.

Mary Elizabeth's stepmother died after only a week in the hospital. Mary Elizabeth plunged into a depression. She cried and lost interest in just about everything including sex. Although I understood her situation, I hated her attitude. I could not muster up any sympathy. After three or four months passed she remained inconsolable. It wasn't reasonable mourning. It was suffering as if she was the first and only young woman to lose a stepmother. Her misery was interfering with my own inner peace. I was distracted on rounds at the hospital. This couldn't continue.

She hadn't been to my apartment since her stepmother died. She rarely called. I reduced my contact with her to infrequently— as infrequently as possible. Finally I made a decision. I had to end it with Mary Elizabeth. I called her on a Saturday afternoon. We had to meet and get this mess over with.

She answered the phone. I said, "Hi, it's Michael. How about I pick you up and we go for a ride. I need to talk with you."

"Yes, I need to talk to you as well," she said and her tone was filled with something I had never heard before. What was it—fear, disdain, regret, loathing? Maybe she was going to save me the effort of breaking it off.

It was a blustery April day. Springtime was resisting arrival. The almost two hour drive was unpleasant but I was feeling good about ending the relationship. When I rang the bell at her home, she opened the door and was already in her coat. No invite in. She pulled the door closed and walked toward my car, which was parked in the driveway under the portico. Her house was huge—a mansion of sorts. She lived close to where Grace Kelly had grown up. Now I was certain she was going to save me the difficulty of breaking up with her. We got into my Monza and drove toward the farm country, west of Roxbury. I was thinking about getting back to life as I had been enjoying it before Mary Elizabeth reinvaded my space. There were several new nurses at the hospital with great bodies and I wanted to go exploring.

"Look, Michael, I don't know how else to do this but to just come out with it. I'm pregnant. It's definitely yours because I haven't been with anyone else."

The statement startled me to the extent that I could still be startled. "You're certain that you're pregnant?"

"Yes, I saw my uncle and he did a test. I'm due in about five months."

"Well, what do you want to do," I said.

"What does that mean?"

"Do you want to have it or do you want to get an abortion?"

"Are you out of your fucking mind? An abortion? I don't want an abortion. I'm going to have this child. Your child."

"No, it's our child."

"Yes, that's what I meant to say—our child."

"Well then I guess we should get married," I said.

"Are you sure? Married?"

"Mary Elizabeth, I'm certainly not sure. But it seems like a reasonable thing to do given the society we live in."

"It certainly will make my father happier."

"Does he know?"

"Of course not. Only my uncle and I and now you know."

"Then let's just elope. I don't want a big deal wedding, and there really isn't enough time anyway."

"I always imagined a big wedding," she said.

"How could that work?" I asked.

"Oh, you're probably right. Let's just get married."

We drove to Maryland the following weekend and were married by a Justice of the Peace. When we drove back to Roxbury, and told her father, he seemed happy.

"Your stepmother would love this," he said. "I wish she were here to see it. She always liked you, Michael." Then he cried. Mary Elizabeth held him and I could see her eyes fill with tears although only a few found there way down her face.

Mary Elizabeth O'Rourke-Ross moved into my NY apartment. She got a job working in the scholarship office at Columbia University. My medical school curriculum continued. Five months later our child was born and you already know what happened.

From the day we married until the day the newborn died, Mary Elizabeth was not interested in sex. Not even in any intimate touches or warm passionate kisses. And after the death of this deformed child, she remained in her sexless agitated state of mind. An unreasonable idea held me captive—that somehow it was her state of mind, the self-pity fueled selfishness and frigidity that appropriately led to a malformed child. How could it lead to anything else? It was during these months following the death of the anencephalic child we were to name Addi that I began to despise Mary Elizabeth O'Rourke. The baby was mine when she found out she was pregnant, but only hers after it died. She would not allow me to comfort her—as if comforting her loss was an impossible task. She made no effort to comfort my sorrow. In fact it didn't appear that she even entertained the idea I might also be saddened over the loss of my daughter. There seemed no point in sharing with her the sights I experienced through the 8X11 window in the delivery room door.

DECEPTION

DECEPTION

Once I completed medical school, there was no time to think of anything but medicine. I was offered an internship and residency at Harlem Hospital Center. A medical resident in the Columbia P&S Department of Medicine at Harlem Hospital Center worked every other night and every other weekend. I worked in excess of one hundred hours per week. The opportunity to avoid spending time with Mary Elizabeth was welcomed. My disdain for her continued to grow. We went to certain necessary social gatherings as husband and wife, but that was it. She had her life and I had mine. Nonetheless it was an odd hatred because I admired her intelligence and her humor, enjoyed dancing with her, even liked her smile. But if I looked at her for longer than a moment, the loathing broke through, similar to the way I could feel compassion for the hopelessly sick drunks and addicts at the hospital, suffering day in and day out with no hope for recovery and then quickly see no future but that suffering and pointless tests that would lead only to death or worse, which is why I continued to use potassium chloride to end this needless suffering. But, it had to be done cautiously. I didn't need some asshole who couldn't understand the clear wisdom behind my decisions to wonder about the rate of death among my patients. So, caution was a priority. Numbers were not important. The task that was important was mercy for those who would suffer most.

At the time, the early work of another physician in New York named Elizabeth Kubler-Ross was becoming known. She wrote about death. She defined the manner in which humans deal with death—denial, anger, bargaining, depression and acceptance. I agreed with what she had to say. I thought every hospital should have some form of help to relieve the suffering of those who were close to death with no hope of recovery. I began to work on this at Harlem Hospital. But most physicians were not ready for it. It was too threatening to their rescue impulses and needs. Still, those suffering at death's door needed a resource to help them in any way possible. I organized an ethics committee. I got the local community interested in forming a hospice organization because there had to be more to it than potassium chloride.

Additionally, during my three years of internal medicine training, I fucked every willing and able female who would have me and I tried to do it well. This earned me an extraordinary reputation—Michael Ross is uninhibited but respectful was the word that spread about. What happened between me and my sex partners was private. But apparently the women talked because there were frequent requests. It was a good thing—all this desired sex, all those horny women. I was very fortunate.

Somewhere during this time I began to feel that I was not giving Mary Elizabeth a fair shake. Why the repeated recurrence of ambivalence? Where was it coming from? Should I make one more effort to convert her to a sex-loving affectionate woman—a woman who at least came close to my expectations of a relationship based on admiration, respect, friendship, and love? I wanted to be faithful to a woman with whom I could share passion and romance. I wanted sweet intimate sex and wild lust-driven fucking. Wild lust-driven fucking is one of the great pleasures of human existence. What was the point in living a life without it? It was attainable. Why not work on Mary Elizabeth's short-comings?

One of my professors was a well respected psychiatrist. I made an appointment to see him and related my story of unsuccessful marriage in detail. He agreed to help. Now, the task was to convince Mary Elizabeth.

"Do you think we have a successful marriage?" I asked her one evening while we sat in the apartment, reading.

"I don't know what a successful marriage is. I mean my married cousins seem to be doing okay. Well, maybe not Regan. Her husband gets drunk and beats her."

"I wasn't asking you to compare. What do you think of our marriage?"

"It's better than Grace's. Her husband is a drunk and they just keep making babies."

"Can't you just look at us? Do we have a successful marriage?"

"I don't know for sure," she said. "Are you happy?"

"Please answer my question, first."

"I don't know because I think, sometimes, that you're not happy."

"Mary Elizabeth, we don't have sex. You never get passionate. You never seduce me. You don't even come to bed with me. You wait for me to fall asleep, first. In the morning, you're in some form of coma because I cannot wake you up. How could I be happy?"

"It all happened after the baby died," she said.

"Not true. It all happened when you were raped at fourteen."

"Did I tell you that?" Her face showed no expression.

I couldn't believe what she had said. "Did you not tell me that?"

"Well, I may have inferred it, but I choose not to talk about it."

"Here's the thing, if you don't do something about it, I am going to leave you. I can't live like this."

She seemed surprised by my comment. She was silent for a moment, twirling her hair in her left thumb and index finger. "What can I do?" she finally said. "What do you want from me? You're a bastard—a heartless bastard." She began to cry.

"One of my professors has a world-wide reputation as a very fine psychiatrist. He has a special interest in young people like us with seemingly overwhelming sex problems. He would probably see you for nothing because I'm an intern at the hospital. Please see him. Please."

Mary Elizabeth began seeing Dr. Marvin Steinway. She went every week on Thursday afternoons. But she became more reticent with me as the weeks and then months passed. Dr. Steinway never said anything to me and Mary Elizabeth never requested my involvement in any of the sessions. After about three months had passed, I ran into Dr. Steinway in the Columbia Presbyterian Medical Center lobby and he smiled at me but kept on walking. Then I heard him call my name.

"Dr. Ross."

I turned toward him.

He walked back to where I was standing, looked around to be sure no one was within earshot. "I haven't seen your wife in over a month. She stopped coming just when I thought we were getting to some important thresholds. See if you can get her to return. I'll hold her appointment time on Thursdays for another week, but if she doesn't show or call, I'm going to have to end working with her."

"Thank you," was all I could manage to say. I was angry and embarrassed.

That evening when I got home there was a surprise waiting for me. The apartment was darkened except for candles that had been lit and placed on tables all over the apartment. As I closed the door, *The Stripper* began playing on the Hi Fi. Mary Elizabeth danced into view in the candlelight wearing a see-through white negligee with a lacey red bra and very skimpy panties visible underneath. Her moves were sexy and seductive and as the music ended the negligee was off. She dropped to her knees in front of me, removed my pants and began sucking my cock. I was turned on until she gagged. I lifted her from her knees and carried her to the sofa where I removed the bra and panties. I made love to her first, and then I fucked her. She made no sounds but I saw a smile appear and then vanish as I came a second time inside of her. The smile was an odd look—self-satisfied—as if she had successfully accomplished a mission.

It had been a long hard week of work and I fell asleep with her in my arms. When I awoke, she was not on the sofa with me. The apartment was dark—no candles still burning. I needed to piss. I went to the bathroom and saw the note on the kitchen table. "MICHAEL, WENT TO A MOVIE. DIDN'T WANT TO WAKE YOU. BE HOME AROUND ELEVEN, ME"

I was confused. Why would she do such a thing? We had made love. She seemed to have overcome some serious problem. Maybe this was why she didn't want to return to see Dr. Steinway. She had conquered her demons. But then why did she leave after the seduction and the lovemaking? Why didn't she stay with me—her lover? And what was that smile about?

I showered and put on a pair of scrubs. There was some leftover Chinese in the refrig. I was heating it up when I heard the key in the front door.

"Hi. I forgot you might be hungry."

"We could have gone out for something to eat," I said. "Why did you leave?"

"I don't know. You were sound asleep and I knew how tired you were, but I needed to do something."

"What did you see?"

"I didn't go to a movie. I just walked along Fifth Avenue and looked in the shop windows. I stopped to get a bite at some little Bistro near Saks. They had delicious pecan pie. Then I took a taxi home."

"Why did you leave? I don't understand."

"You know, Michael, I'm not like you. I don't have answers for everything I do. I just needed to be alone and have some time to think or something."

"Are you alright?" I asked.

"I'm fine. Now eat your food. I'm going to read."

I sat alone at the kitchen table. She sat in the rocking chair in the living room. She was reading an essay by Virginia Woolf, something about having your own room.

I didn't mention the episode to Dr. Steinway. Why bother. Mary Elizabeth was a master of deceit when it came to inner feelings. She deceived herself as much or more than she deceived me. After I finished the Kung Po chicken I watched "The Seven Samurai" and fell asleep again on the sofa.

Two months later, it was November, she told me she was pregnant. There had been no sex after the 'Stripper' night. Mostly, she read and painted horses and humpback whales using oil on enormous canvases. She visited her father and lunched with girlfriends from college. Rarely, she visited me at the hospital when I was on call and ate with me in the Doctors' Dining Room. My colleagues thought she was charming. "Your wife is lovely," they would say. "Such a smart young woman." But inside of me a wildfire was beginning. It was an under-burn about to explode into an inferno.

A WEE LITTLE ONE

A WEE LITTLE ONE

"So, Michael me Darlin Boy," she said putting on that brogue I once loved to hear, "what shall we call this wee little one?"

I didn't expect the question. It came out of nowhere. It was February and very cold in New York City. My misery and helplessness were so thick I had almost forgotten about the baby. My mind was on the war in South East Asia—a means of escape from Mary Elizabeth.

Although a very tough hombre, I'm also a romantic and that side of me was dying—smothered by Mary Elizabeth's cold deceptive heart, or perhaps by my own expectations. But the arrival of this little child had become lost in my anger and self-pity. Mary Elizabeth's question reminded me and brought a sense of anticipation and excitement. I was to be a father—have a child to love. But then I remembered Addi. Would this little one be healthy? It had to be healthy.

"Michael, if it's a boy, after me and my Dad. And if it's a girl, how about Mackenzie? I love that name."

"Sounds good to me," she said. "What about middle names?"

"I don't know. You pick the middle names."

"I'll think about some," she said.

Mackenzie Claire was born in May of 1969—a perfectly formed adorable girl-child. And the smile she gave me when I first held her in the delivery room captured my heart forever.

I completed my residency in July and went back on active duty. They promoted me to major. We moved into base housing at Eglin Air Force Base.

"I don't understand," Mary Elizabeth said. "If your in the Army, why do we live on an air force base?"

I had to answer the question carefully. "My unit is temporarily assigned here for training," I said. "Just enjoy living in Florida. Think of how cold it will get up north, and how pleasant it will remain here."

"Why do you need to be in the military, anyway? You're a Columbia trained physician. We could live in New York City, or Westchester, or even Connecticut instead of this Florida shithole."

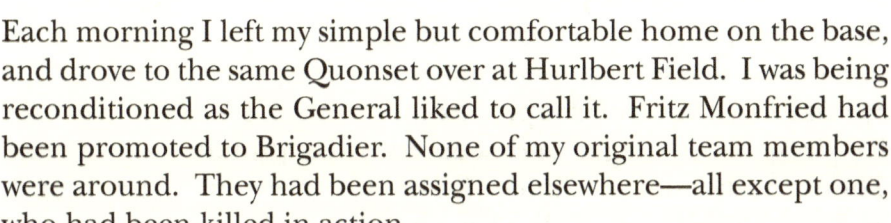

Each morning I left my simple but comfortable home on the base, and drove to the same Quonset over at Hurlbert Field. I was being reconditioned as the General liked to call it. Fritz Monfried had been promoted to Brigadier. None of my original team members were around. They had been assigned elsewhere—all except one, who had been killed in action.

So now I was the older guy with experience. I was "reconditioned" for three days a week, and worked in the base clinic two days a week. I had the weekends off to spend with Mary Elizabeth and my daughter, Mackenzie. I did not get deployed.

After three months of this routine, I was ordered to meet with the General on a Saturday morning in his office at the Quonset. When I arrived, everything but the front door had been boarded up. The few signs that had been on the building were gone, and only the General's staff car was there, the driver leaning on it and smoking a cigarette. When he saw me he dropped the cigarette, braced and saluted. "Sir," he said. "The General is inside."

"Thank You, Sergeant," I said, returning his salute.

I walked in through the front door and Monfried was seated at his desk puffing on a cigar.

"Major Ross, come on in and have a seat. Meet Tom Reynolds, He's with the CIA. Just relax. Let's make this an informal meeting."

Reynolds was wearing cheap gray slacks that looked like work pants with baggy pockets, and a faded blue short-sleeve polo. He had sneakers on his feet.

After I sat, the General continued, "I guess you've noticed we're closing up shop here at Hurlbert." He exhaled a large cloud of thick smoke from what looked like a pricey cigar. "Our remaining teams have been absorbed into what is now called Special Operations Group. No more Special Warfare Teams." He drew on the cigar and seemed to be thinking about that. Then another large cloud of smoke came out of his mouth and nose, this time. "I don't have to remind you that all of this is classified. Anyway, my plans for you to be one of our docs, obviously have changed." He looked down at the floor, then at his cigar. "But the good news is that you may be exactly what the CIA is looking for to fill a slot over in Vietnam. I've been telling Tom about you and your early missions with us. I'll let him continue."

"Major, you sound like the exact man we need. The Army is willing to lend you to us."

"He's right, Mike," the General interrupted, "You're perfect for this assignment."

"CIA needs someone who can travel to villages in Vietnam without arousing suspicion. Someone savvy enough to notice signs of VC or NVA activity in a village. Because you're a doc, you could provide medical care to the villagers. We have been doing this for several years, now, as a gesture of good will toward the South Vietnamese villagers. But if in the course of your doctoring, you happened to notice things that your experience would allow you to notice, you'd report this back to us, and we would use that information to facilitate a faster end to this war."

"What unit would I be with over there?"

"We'd assign you to some local Army unit in the area of operations. But the unit CO would know that you were working with us and not under his command. There would be no specifics about what you were actually doing. We don't want you connected with Special Ops or even that you're an Airborne Ranger. You'll just be an Army doc doing local village rounds. You'll have plenty of supplies to care for the villagers and earn their trust. That way it would be unlikely for you to arouse suspicion and put yourself at excessive risk."

I looked at him and smiled. "Excessive risk? I thrive on excessive risk."

The General smiled and kept puffing on his cigar so that the room looked like it was enveloped in fog.

"Sounds like an interesting job," I said. But I was thinking of what a perfect escape this would be from Mary Elizabeth. I'd miss my daughter, but not my wife. I was back to full blown rage and hatred. She had no respect for my military career and no interest in love-making or passion.

I accepted the assignment. It was a one year duty station. Mary Elizabeth was very happy to return to our New York apartment. I went to Vietnam in early December, just in time for the monsoon rains. I had wanted her to move back into an apartment my parents had in their house, mostly for Mackenzie's sake, but the Ice Queen wanted to be in that 87th street co-op. Mary Elizabeth did not like my parents. I think she was recognizing that they could see through her manipulative bullshit. They knew she was cold because of her behavior with me. She was not affectionate. She rarely even touched me—held a hand or rested her head on me, gave me a little loving peck.

She went to graduate school. Columbia accepted her in a Master's program in English Literature. My folks took care of Mackenzie when Mary Elizabeth was at school.

From time to time, she sent me cassette tapes of Mackenzie gibbering. She could say 'Dada' before I returned home. But there were no letters from Mary Elizabeth. No words of love or longing or lonliness.

I did my job. Visited many villages every week. When something looked suspicious; wood from ammunition boxes cut up and stacked for firewood or ground that had been heavily tracked on near a pile of manure because there was probably a tunnel entrance or a big hole filled with munitions and weapons under the manure pile—I'd report this to Tom Reynolds. I was assigned to the First Air Calvary Division in II Corps—a place called Phuoc Vinh. I had a jeep and driver, and even access to a helicopter available for my travel needs.

I was helping sick villagers and saving lives. It seemed the NVA and VC allowed me free movement throughout the country side. I always had plenty of antibiotics and pain medication as well as soup and milk powder to give away. I wore standard issue jungle fatigues and wore the First Calvary patch on my sleeve. I did carry a 45 side arm and an M16 just in case. And I had a special issue knife with an eight inch razor-sharp double blade. I carried it in a sheath that was strapped to my right thigh, and reachable through a hole in my right pants pocket—just in case. But in all of my doctoring visits I never had to fire a shot and I was never attacked.

Nonetheless, I missed combat. I was an Airborne Ranger, a skilled warrior. I missed combat action. On one visit after about five months in country, I told Reynolds how much I missed combat.

"I'll bet those teams could use my first hand guidance when they visit a village where I've already been," I said.

"Yeah but Doc, you're a Doc now. You can't get involved in combat."

"Yes I can. They go in at night, right. So I darken my face. I don't speak. I'm just a skilled gun with first-hand information. If I were a team leader, I'd love to have such an asset along," I said.

Actually, the MAC-V SOG Lt Colonel who headed up the SOG teams in II and III Corps loved the idea. It was amusing that the Military people considered me CIA, and the CIA people considered me military. I was a man without a home. Until the teams saw me at work. I was a highly skilled warrior. I had the advantage over most highly skilled warriors, however. I could kill and save lives.

By June of 1970, my sixth month, I was going on night raids as a routine. I became the sixth man in the usual five man teams. I killed with my knife, a garrote, or a 9mm Browning High Power pistol. There was something very special about lifting a scumbag communist terrorist off his feet with thirty inches of sharp steel piano wire around his neck.

During a medical visit to a village in III corps in early August, I noticed a small but fit Vietnamese woman whose face I recognized from some photos I had seen during a visit with Reynolds. He was showing me most wanted VC. This woman had killed many US soldiers during the Tet offensive in Hue. She'd pretend to be a peasant woman with a dead baby. She would hold what appeared to be an infant wrapped in soiled blankets and cry out for help. When a soldier ran to help her, she would shoot him in the face and then disappear into a doorway.

I reported her presence in the village and went with the team on the night raid. Killing her stayed with me—her pissing herself as her body trembled, hanging from my garrote as it cut into her trachea and carotid arteries. She was small and light so I lifted her at least a foot off the floor with the wire. I whispered in her ear as she gurgled and sprayed blood, from her lacerated neck, "This is for the ones you shot in the face in Hue, you bitch-cunt."

I still carry a scar and a barely noticeable limp from that encounter because she had a knife and was tough enough to slip it out from under her clothing and plunge it into my right hip as I held her up off the floor, killing her with my garrote. Bone stopped her knife and so it did little damage except for the infection that would follow. I didn't release any pressure or lower her when she stabbed me. I intensified the pressure so that her blood sprayed all over the hut walls, bedding, and my arms and hands—all over the pictures she had sitting on a small box next to her bed. "Fuck you," I hissed as I released her lifeless body and it folded to the floor.

I removed the knife and saw that a quarter inch of the tip was not there. Using my fingers, it was palpable in my right hip bone.

I said nothing until back in Phuoc Vinh. Next morning a Huey flew me down to the 19th Surgical Hospital Unit were I was treated. They removed the knife tip and gave it to me as a memento. But infection set in and worsened. I was evacuated to Hawaii—Tripler Army Hospital—in late August of 1970.

Two months of intravenous antibiotics cleared the infection. Then came orders for a two week leave and a date to report to Fort Hamilton, in Brooklyn, for further orders. A limp was quite noticeable at the time due to some bone inflammation from the infection and I required a crutch to reduce weight bearing. Nonetheless, this mostly disappeared with time. There was no pain and only slight limitation of motion.

STATUS QUO

STATUS QUO

During the several months at Tripler, Mary Elizabeth did not visit me. My parents did, and they brought Mackenzie. When she first saw me, she looked at my picture, which she was still carrying and then at me. A smile rose on her face like a sunrise, she dropped the picture, and reached for me. She was almost a year and a half old. "Dada, Dada," she said as her head rested down on my left shoulder. She was beautiful and she loved me.

My parents stayed for several weeks. I returned to the Continental US in time to enjoy Thanksgiving and Christmas with Mackenzie and my parents. Mary Elizabeth was standoffish when I first saw her. I had taken a taxi from the airport to my co-op. She was sleeping when I arrived home. I heard Mackenzie babbling in her crib. She was talking to Churchill. He licked me till my face needed a washing, whining with pleasure the whole time. Mary Elizabeth slept through it all. When I finally woke her up with a kiss on the lips and a hug, she pulled back from me, and said, "Oh Hi," with the hint of a smile on her face. The sad part was that she was pretty, even in the morning, even with no make-up, of which she wore very little. But she was missing a heart.

Several nights later, with no sex offered by Mary Elizabeth, or desired by me from her, I told her I was going to a reunion with some of my friends from the Columbia P&S training program I had completed. Actually I called a playboy bunny I had dated before Mary Elizabeth came back on the scene. We spent the night in bed at her apartment. She was a magnificent sex partner. She taught me some fine ways to please a woman. And as usual, she had a treat for me as a welcome home present.

"Have you ever fucked a girl up the ass?" she asked after we had recovered from round three of love-making.

"No. Actually, I've been a bit resistant to the idea."

"Why?"

"Seems like it might hurt and besides the other function of the orifice in question might be a bit of a turn-off," I said,

She laughed. "Oh you poor misled little fellow," she said and slipped up onto her knees. Her firm 36 Bs hung perfectly from her chest. Her nipples were erect and she began to suck my cock into hardness. "Now," she said once I was up and firm again, "Put it in my ass." She turned around. "Fuck me up the ass, Michael. Please fuck me up the ass."

She said it with excited anticipation and pressed her perfect ass into my cock. As always she smelled lovely—some expensive scent. It was the tightest hole I'd ever had my dick in, and she moaned and pushed herself back into me in perfect rhythm. Her little buttocks flattened slightly against each thrust and after several minutes she had a grand orgasm, at which point I let myself come inside of her.

Without uncoupling, she turned her head slightly to look at me and said, "What do you think? Want to do that again before you leave?"

Yes, Bonnie Lee Barnes, the brunette Bunny with the perfect little nose and full lips was a magnificent life-saver. I felt welcomed home. We fell asleep for several hours from exhaustion. When we awoke, we showered together and got in one more fuck after I soaped her and gently washed her pussy into another orgasm.

I had an appointment in Washington D.C. at 3pm. That's what the orders I had picked up at Fort Hamilton said. I didn't know the Army's plans for me since the wound and surgery and the infection. It didn't look like I would have any handicap, just the slightest hint of an uneven gait when I walked fast, and my run was slower than it had been before the infection. I no longer possessed running back or linebacker speed. Would they discharge me, or give me options?

I got to the apartment around seven in the morning. As usual Mary Elizabeth was sleeping. Mackenzie was not in the apartment. I called my mother.

"Well, what a pleasure," she said. I got to keep my granddaughter last night. But Mary Elizabeth never even called me, so I was worried. But when you didn't call, I figured all was okay. It isn't as if she's never done it before."

"She has forgotten to pick up Mackenzie in the past?"

"Michael, I don't want to cause any more problems for you and Mary Elizabeth, but she probably forgot to pick up Mackenzie at least a dozen times while you were away. I mean if she would just call because we worry."

"Why didn't you ever say anything about it to her?"

"I did. She would apologize and say she was forgetful, or had a lot on her mind. She'd always say she knew Mackenzie was in good hands."

"And why didn't you ever tell me?"

"Michael, you had enough on your mind over there—in that terrible war."

"Well, are you going to be around today, or should I get her to come and pick up Mackenzie?"

"No, no. I'll keep her till you get back from Washington. When will you be back?"

"How about I come for supper tonight and sleep over? Then, I'll take Mackenzie home with me in the morning."

"Oh, your Dad and I would love it."

By now, I think my mom knew that Mary Elizabeth was not all she had hoped or imagined. Nonetheless, she was my wife and my mother honored marriage. This is likely why she would not share negative thoughts about Mary Elizabeth with me beyond what she had said in our telephone conversation that morning.

I still did not understand why I was with Mary Elizabeth other than that I had impregnated her and married her as the right thing to do. But it was becoming more difficult as the years passed. Why didn't I leave her after Addi died? Perhaps I had a need to protect. My mother seemed to seek protection from me when I was just a small boy—protection from her husband, my father. And what about Bruce? She had made me feel responsible for protecting him. But then why did my mother marry my dad in the first place? Life seemed too great a mystery.

The idea of love shouldn't be that difficult, if it is in fact a real entity. But when I subjected it to deconstruction it seemed to add up to need, hormones, desire, and lust. Wasn't it all about propagation of the species? It wasn't mystical. The humans who experienced these feelings of need and desire multiplied. It's Darwinism at work. And then these little ones needed to be protected in order to survive. No, there is no mystique here. Maybe love as we dream of it and speak of it is all an illusion—all just bullshit. Maybe I had to stop wasting time and effort on the illusion. But then I'd think of Lovey and confusion would reign again.

I didn't even wake Mary Elizabeth, I shit, showered, again, and shaved. I still had the scent of Bonnie Lee on me and it was distracting. Before I left in my Class A uniform, my hat with all the gold on the brim, I left a note for Mary Elizabeth—told her she didn't have to worry about Mackenzie and that I was taking the car and would bring Mackenzie home the next day. I didn't sign it.

MAKING CHANGES

MAKING CHANGES

The Eastern Electra flight was noisy but fast. The Monza convertible was parked at Newark Airport. Mary Elizabeth had banged it up terribly in my absence so a few more door-dings in the airport parking lot were of little consequence. There would be dinner and a warm bed for the night when I returned from DC. I'd head back to the city the following morning with Mackenzie.

During the flight, which was like sitting in a vibrating chair, I considered my career options. I could insist on another assignment with the Medical Corps and probably get it. Yes, somewhere that had no graduate education available for Mary Elizabeth. Or, I could get an assignment out of the country, again. Probably not in a war zone because of my hip, but someplace where dependents couldn't go. But I rejected this option because I no longer trusted Mary Elizabeth with Mackenzie. When we had talked about my trip to Washington, Mary Elizabeth warned me that she was tiring of my military career. "You better make some changes, buster. You better make some changes," is what she had screamed at me a few days before I decided to meet Bonnie Lee Barnes.

It was raining and cold in D.C. when I arrived. A call to a friend who worked in the Forrestal Building before I left New

York City had informed me about the lousy weather. My military trench coat with the lining buttoned in did the trick. It was a short taxi ride from Washington National to the Forrestal Building. An elevator carried me to the fifth floor. Signs with arrows were clear to various room numbers. My destination was room 5210. The room number was on the door, but no other descriptive appeared on the wall to the right or left of the door as with most of the other offices I had passed.

I turned the knob and entered a small office with plenty of fluorescent lighting and a pair of square windows that did not appear to open. A wrinkled older man, somewhere, I'd estimate, in his fifties, sat at the large steel desk centered in the room. He was wearing a wrinkled gray suit, a wrinkled off-white dress shirt and a wrinkled red tie. There was one metal arm chair facing the desk and the windows. The desk faced the only apparent door through which I had just entered. Another smaller gray metal chair was in a corner to the right of the door as you entered. There were no file cabinets and no visible telephones. The floor was tiled with some sort of gray industrial vinyl. The room looked like a large storage closet.

"And you are?" the man asked.

"Major Ross, Sir." I didn't know whether he was military but simply used the polite and safe response.

"Yes, I've been expecting you. Take off your coat and hat and put them on that other chair. Don't worry about the dripping," he said. "Have a seat," and he gestured to the chair facing his desk.

Since I had entered, he never seemed to look me in the eye. He looked past me and around me and behind me, but never directly at me. I heard a click that sounded like the door had just locked. I think I sat up straighter and must have looked surprised.

"That door locks electronically. I don't want anyone walking in on this conversation. This is a safe room. Do you understand?"

"Yes, Sir, I do." It seemed like my military career was always classified.

"Good, then let's get started. I am with the CIA. It is my understanding from speaking with your superiors that the Army is willing to discharge you from active duty if you are interested in taking the position I am about to offer you. You've worked with us and for us in the past when you were last in Southeast Asia and before that, in your Special Warfare Team activities based out of Hurlbert. We've been impressed by your courage and mission orientation. You get the job done effectively and efficiently. So, I will cut to the chase. We need someone who is willing and capable of doing some periodic clean-up work. Fast little jobs—a few weeks at most—where information is provided and a smart tactical mind can use it to accomplish a mission. Do you understand?"

"Are you describing assassination work?"

He still was not looking at me, but his tone lowered and seemed agitated, "We don't use that word any longer in the United States because we do not approve of assassinations or assassins. We prefer individually accomplished clean-up work or finders work. We refer to those who do it for us as resources, and assets. You would be a perfect resource because as a physician on vacation, or on some kind of missionary work, for example, you could do this clean-up work for us with a very low degree of suspicion. You could go about your business and your life and simply take trips to hunt or fish from time to time. Do you see my point?"

"Yes. I enjoy hunting and fishing," I said, "all sorts of fish and game. How and what will you pay me for my services?"

He looked me in the eye for the first time. "We will reimburse all of your expenses, pay for first class travel and accommodations, plus we will deposit a minimum of twenty-thousand dollars in a Swiss bank account for each job. It's a piece-work kind of contract with no specific endpoint. You may resign once you have completed a minimum of five years with us. Every five years we will renegotiate your contract. There will be no record of your working for us nor will you ever disclose that you work for us. We will deny any association suggested. We know you can do this job or we would not be offering it, and you already have a very high security clearance. You come strongly recommended for this work by several of your former commanders and associates. Your reputation in Southeast Asia is near folklore. You were known as 'The Serpent,' were you not?"

"I'm not familiar with that name, Sir, nor to what you are referring."

He smiled. "Yes, you understand this setup perfectly. Do we have a deal?"

"Yes," I said. "I accept your offer." I knew there would never be any record of this conversation, or any written contract. In my new line of work, such records did not exist.

"So, let's work out a few basic details," he said. Doctors have pagers, correct?" He did not give me a chance to answer him. "Pagers," he added and handed me a small black and chrome one. It was slightly larger than most I had seen in length and thickness, but was thinner from side to side. "This has a magnificent range. It will work in most places on this planet. It will also work for service or hospital calls to contact you. You simply need to give them the phone number on the device. We will contact you via another internal receiver. Only we know that number. When we call you it will sound like this." The pager beeped a repetitive triplet tone. "If anyone else calls the number on the device it will sound like this." The device beeped a repetitive single tone. "Clever, no?" he said.

But I still had a few questions. "What about my discharge from Active Duty?"

"Consider it done. You will receive notice of the separation process beginning by letter next week. All significant parties have agreed to this provided you agreed to what we discussed today. We do want you to remain a reservist, as long as you work for us. There will be no reserve obligations, but we may occasionally use reserve training as a cover to get you from one place to another. We will see to it that you are always assigned to an appropriate reserve unit."

Was it difficult to find sane people willing to kill as a matter of assignment—as if being asked to go to a file drawer and pull out a particular file? I had proven that I could do it. Killing was not a big deal to me. People make choices in their lives and sometimes these choices bring them great success, and sometimes the choices get them killed. There are some people who must be killed to protect the innocent. It's a simple reality. Fairness and justice don't always get things accomplished in the best and most necessary manner. And since there is no god, someone needs to take the responsibility.

There was no paperwork to fill out or sign. The CIA knew how to reach me. I had the pager. They had the information they needed about me from my military file.

The man seated across the desk from me stopped speaking. He was looking at me with a smirk-like smile. He had never offered a name and I knew better than to ask. Assets are not employees.

"Is that it, then?" I asked.

"I think so," he said.

The less I knew the less of a problem I could be if I 'turned' for any reason. But one thing did occur to me in the moment.

"Am I free to live and travel wherever I wish? And how do I contact you or whomever if I need to for any reason?"

"Just make sure you have the pager with you and you can go anywhere. We can change the code so it works anyplace on the planet. A contact person will be in touch with you within a few weeks."

That was it. He stood up and I stood up. No further words, no smiles, no hand shake.

I took the shuttle back to Newark and drove to my parents' home. Mackenzie ran down the hallway from the kitchen to the front door when she heard my voice. It was the same hallway I had run down as a little boy when I heard my father's voice. But my dad was a laborer. I was now a hired killer and soon, hopefully, a hired healer as well. The irony began to rise in my consciousness—a physician and an assassin—but then I saw my daughter's upraised arms and she was all I could think about.

"Hello Mackenzie. I missed you."

"Dada fly," she said.

"Yes, Daddy was on an airplane."

She pointed up. "Apa," she said, "Apa."

My mom had made a fresh pot of coffee and a pot roast. Dad had his gallon of zinfandel out and on the kitchen floor by his chair at the head of the table. In those days zinfandel was not yet glorified by whomever was responsible for the glorification of wine. It was a cheap California red with a bit more alcohol than most red wines. It was fruity and good with everything but fish. That was my father's opinion. Mom liked a glass of water or a cup of coffee with her meals. I only enjoyed coffee after a meal or with breakfast. But I had developed a taste for that zinfandel.

"Michael, want a Manhattan? We have good reason to celebrate your safe return," my dad said. "What is going to happen now?"

"Well, I am done with active military duty," I said.

"Great news," Mom said. "And by the way, will you join us for Thanksgiving and or Christmas?"

"Okay, let's have a Manhattan," I said. "And I'll let you know about the holidays. I'd love to join the family for both. Can we invite Mary Elizabeth's father?"

"Of course. He's welcome to both parties," Mom said.

Mackenzie galloped around us saying "mana, mana." My mother and father put their arms around me and I held them tightly. Mackenzie wrapped her arms around my leg and repeated, "Dada."

I spent the night with my parents. Mackenzie and I slept in the guest room with the two single beds on the second floor. By nine the next morning we were headed back to the City. I was thinking about the conversation I'd had with my father after the Manhattans and the zinfandel the night before. Mother was putting Mackenzie to bed. I'd washed the dinner dishes.

"I don't know how I'm going to stick it out with Mary Elizabeth," I had said. "We don't have much in common except for some good political discussions and our mutual love of music."

"It's probably just as hard for her. Look at it that way."

"I don't think so. She doesn't seem to be interested."

"Then why the hell did you marry her?" he had said.

"Now you know the answer to that one, Dad." And I raised my eyebrows.

"Okay, but you better figure something out before it's too late."

"When will it be too late?"

"I'm not sure," he said. "But you'll know."

"When was it too late for you?"

"I love your mother," he said, and downed his fourth glass of zinfandel with one long swallow.

Now, as the Monza cruised through the Lincoln Tunnel into Manhattan my mind was rushing through the past as if to find some answer, some missing link to this mess with Mary Elizabeth. How could marriage work with us? I hated her. "But what about Mackenzie?" my mother had asked when she returned from the kitchen and figured out the gist of the conversation my father and I were having. That was the key question. What about Mackenzie? I looked at my daughter sitting in the tan leather bucket seat beside me. She was fancying the lights along the walls of the tunnel, mesmerized by their rhythmic passing.

The passing opaque light-covers reminded me of the flickering projection of an old silent movie. My mind began trying to unwind from Vietnam—trying to leave the wild adventures and the killing behind, frame by frame. It wasn't an easy transition. What would I do with my new life? My military career was over. The future with the CIA was a mystery—what, exactly, it would involve. But I had a medical degree—well trained in Internal Medicine. I had the apartment in Manhattan. Mary Elizabeth was still in school. Maybe I'd do a fellowship at Columbia, or perhaps I could get a teaching position. There were plenty of pussy resources in the City. Maybe I needed to slow down and take a good hard look before making any other major changes.

AN ASSET

AN ASSET

I never suffered from cold feet, had nerves of steel. I knew this from my military experiences—the ambushes and raids—hunting and being hunted. Had they seen it in that psychological profile back in college? What could they have learned from all that expressed anger, disregard, and disrespect? Was this the reason they had been so interested in training me to be a stealthy extraordinary killer? This question was swimming around in my mind one cold November afternoon while looking out my window at some kids playing on 87th. A light snow had fallen during the early morning hours. Christmas was slightly over a month away. We spent Thanksgiving alone in the apartment because Mary Elizabeth didn't feel like seeing my family. I cooked a turkey for us and David O'Rourke joined us. I had some money in the bank so I could buy something nice for Mackenzie from Santa Claus, but just wasn't sure what it would be.

The cold weather made my hip hurt and this put me in an unpleasant mood. Mary Elizabeth had taken Mackenzie to visit her father over in Pennsylvania and then went to study with her friend Eleanor, whom I was convinced was a lesbian, even though she was married with a child. Maybe Mary Elizabeth was a lesbian. Maybe that was the reason for her coldness. Or maybe it was me. But then why did all of my fucking partners come back for more? They seemed satisfied.

Before I switched mental gears and explored my medical career options, the pager interrupted my thoughts. It beeped in a repetitive triplet monotone. Since receiving it, I kept it on or near me. The tone that said my new employer was calling surprised me, but it also pleased me. Perhaps there would be some excitement in my immediate future. There was a local New York number in the display.

I used my home phone and dialed. A male voice answered, "This is Mr. Jones."

"Yes, this is Michael Ross," I said.

"Yes, Dr. Ross, I'm calling to arrange a lunch meeting with you. Perhaps tomorrow?"

It was Friday. There were no plans with Mary Elizabeth for Saturday, and frankly, the less I saw of her the better. "Sure, tomorrow. Where and when?"

"There's a small Greek restaurant at 10th avenue and 49th. It's called Jimmy the Greek's. How about 1pm?"

"I'll be there. How will I know you?"

"You won't need to. I'll know you," he said. "I remember you from Hawaii. We were at Tripler around the same time. You probably don't remember me."

There were many faces from Tripler that formed a blur in my memory but the CIA had the special beeper number. This Mr. Jones had called me on that line. The one for my medical work, I had given to no one as yet, and the other was a CIA exclusive. So who was this Mr. Jones? Would he be my contact person? I did not recall meeting anyone named Jones during my stay in Hawaii.

"Well, I'm looking forward to meeting you, tomorrow," I added.

"Fine, we can discuss the details of that fishing trip you wrote me about. See you then," he said followed by the familiar click of a call that has ended.

Not only did I not recall any Mr. Jones at Tripler, but also couldn't remember discussing fishing trips while in Hawaii. Fishing trips came up in conversation with fishing buddies, the few I had, and with Harry, a fellow who tied flies at Abercrombie's on Madison Avenue where I usually bought my flies. Harry had fished many fine trout streams in the Northeast. He was particularly fond of the East Branch of the Delaware and the Pequest—the former in New York and the latter in New Jersey. I frequently fished both rivers with patterns he had tied.

Did the CIA know I was a fly fisherman? They likely knew many things about me. They never would have hired me to be an asset without knowing a great deal about me. The military had done an extensive file on me, my family, my friends and associates. At one point I recall a fellow from Army Intelligence responsible for checking me out, warning me about whoring. "You need to be careful about what you say when you are fucking," he had said. "Maybe, you need to be careful about who you are fucking. This country has enemies who will stop at nothing to get information that could compromise our efforts to make this a better planet. You need to be careful!" he had said back when I was with the team. But here was the thing; I did not drink much, ever, and I was always careful who I fucked. I had discriminating taste. Fucking a total stranger was no longer my usual way. Several Playboy Bunnies, some coeds, a few nurses, and two or three of the wives of several friends and associates had been my primary sex partners over those years. These were all lovely ladies looking for some recreation and exercise. There was no harm in it that was apparent to me.

Have I mentioned my German Shepherd Dog? His name was Churchill. I thought there was some irony to naming my keen Kraut dog, Churchill. He was a white German Shepherd—rare. Protecting Mary Elizabeth when she was alone in my apartment was the initial idea, but he formed a magnificent bond with Mackenzie. When she slept he was on the floor beside her bed. No one got into the apartment unless I or Mary Elizabeth said it was okay. He was more protective of Mackenzie than he was of Mary Elizabeth. Churchill would attack anyone if I commanded him. Teaching him this skill set was easy. A good Kraut dog will always obey his master.

One night Mary Elizabeth and I were out walking Churchill in the Park. I had to step into the bushes to empty my bladder. Some druggies tried to attack Mary Elizabeth and take her shoulder purse. Churchill bit them badly. They both tried to run off but were easily caught by a mounted policeman who heard the snarling and barking during the attack. I was running after them and Churchill had one of them by the arm, while I dropped the other and dislocated his shoulder. The two were on the ground screaming when the policeman road up on his horse. Churchill was standing over one, snarling and biting every time he tried to move.

He was written up in the NY Mirror, picture and all, for his great work at protecting Mary Elizabeth. She framed the picture and hung it in our sitting room—Mary Elizabeth seated and Churchill sitting beside her with keen ears and eyes.

My point in bringing up Churchill, now, is that he was a magnificent chick magnet. When I walked him in Central Park, good looking girls often stopped to ask his name, tell me how beautiful he was and ask if they could pet him. But I never tried to fuck any of them. They were strangers.

The following day I met Mr. Jones at Jimmy the Greeks on 10th Avenue. He was a large fellow, tall and overweight, wearing a top coat and a fedora. He had a black scarf around his neck. He was sitting at one of the ten or twelve tables in the place. It was in the back, but he sat facing the door. When I walked in after seeing no one who looked likely for a CIA lunch-mate outside, he was waving his fedora to beckon me to his table. I arrived at exactly 1pm.

The place smelled of cumin, oregano, roasted chicken and garlic. There was a hot food bar with a server behind it. A few ceiling fans rotated slowly, keeping the air well-blended. And the tables were glass topped and clean—the kind you usually see in ice cream parlors. I think better on a full stomach. A few stuffed grape leaves and some curried mutton stew appealed to me.

"Good afternoon," I said and set my plate in the center of the table and offered this Mr. Jones a fork. A cup of black coffee sat in front of him.

"No thanks," he said. "I never touch foreign food. Especially not in a dive like this one."

"Smells good and looks clean," I said, looking directly at his face. His eyes were darting all over the room. He looked agitated and nervous. Not what I had expected. He had instructed me in the verbal exchange we just had over the phone the day before.

"Look, I need to give you some information. I have to make sure you were not followed and that we are not being watched," he said.

"Who would want to follow me? I'm just an Army doc, home from the war and awaiting my discharge papers. There is no history worthy of inquiry or attention."

"You never know what the other side knows," he said.

"What other side?" At this point I honestly thought this fellow was an asshole. Had I made a mistake?

"Look, I'm not the usual guy who does this kind of shit," he said.

"What kind of shit?"

Now he looked directly at me, and half smiled. "I'm acting like a jerk, right?"

"Yep, a jerk."

"Okay, I'm supposed to tell you that you need to visit the Abercrombie and Fitch store on Madison and buy ½ dozen custom-made Pale Evening Duns for Crompton Creek. You need to do it today before five pm." As he spoke, he held his hat over his mouth so no one could read his lips.

"Are you making this shit up?" I said although I did understand that certain things should not be said over phone lines that were not secure.

"No, those were my orders."

The grape leaves and mutton were delicious. The jumpy messenger left before I finished my food.

I walked across town on 48th to Madison and then down to the Abercrombie and Fitch store which was on the corner of

45th, arriving just before 3pm. Everything in the place was top of the line. They had outfitted the latest Everest Team, the famous Kon Tiki expedition across the Pacific and Sir Edmund Hillary's Everest expedition. Teddy Roosevelt and Ernest Hemingway had used the outfitting services for fishing and hunting trips. My only Harris Tweed jacket and my Rolex were purchased at the store along with several boxes of wet and dry flies used when fly-fishing for trout. The elevator was a fast ride to the 8th floor where the fly-tying department was located. Harry was not there but there was another fellow behind the counter.

"I'm looking for some custom made Pale Evening Duns tied for Crompton Creek," I said.

He looked at me for five or six seconds and then said, "How many would you like?"

"Half dozen," I said.

"Sorry, but we only sell the custom tied flies by the dozen."

"Okay. How much are they by the dozen?"

"Three dollars and a half."

"May I see the flies?"

He brought out a small finely finished wooden box about half the size of a cigar box. It had a thick sliding lid which he gently withdrew to reveal dozens of perfectly tied Pale Evening Duns separated by compartments in the box according to the fly size, from twelve all the way down to twenty-twos. It looked like Harry's work.

"Did Harry tie these?" I asked.

"Do you know Harry?" he said.

"Yes. We often talk about two of our favorite rivers."

"Jim told me to expect you, today. He's another of our fly tiers. You may enjoy talking to him as well. Why don't you wander down a flight to the gunroom and Jim will find you there. And by the way, that box of flies is for you—no charge."

Abercrombie's was a magnificent establishment for sportsmen. Their clothing was definitely my style and owning one of their shotguns and one of their fly rods would suit me. A famous Italian shotgun maker was the designer and producer of one line of their shotguns. A fellow named Rizzini. I was holding a side by side 28 gauge model, stroking the smooth polished walnut stock as I might the skin of a beautiful woman, when a small man with dark hair in a three piece dark brown wool suit appeared next to me. He had approached quietly and my attention was on the shotgun, which not only had a beautiful wood stock, but also grand balance.

"That's a fine upland bird gun," he said.

"Yes, a beauty. Perhaps one day I'll own one."

"I'm Jim." He extended his hand.

"You don't look like you've been tying flies," I said, as we shook hands.

He smiled. "Come with me."

I followed him into a small recess off the seventh floor showroom and sales area. We took an up elevator and when the doors opened we were in an elegantly appointed office somewhere in the upper levels of the building. Wood was everywhere, bookshelves, desk, chairs, cabinets, gun cases, rod cases, and walls. And on those luxurious wood paneled walls were pictures of many famous people including Hemingway and Sir Edmund Hillary. But there were no pictures of Jim. There was a fireplace and two brown leather wing chairs faced the hearth. A fire was burning quietly behind a sturdy brass and black mesh screen. The room was comfortably warm.

"Have a seat, Michael." He pointed casually to one of the chairs facing the desk. He sat behind the desk. "You'll know me as Jim. We'll always meet here. It's a safe place and you've been coming here for many years so there should be no suspicion. If I need you, I may send you what appears to be a special Abercrombie promotion to a valued customer. You'll recognize it to be from me because there will be one of three, shall we call them code-words, on the envelope, which will always be the same yellow as this envelope. The words are Pale, Evening, and Dun." He removed a large yellow envelope from a leather attaché case which he lifted from the floor beside his chair. The case was well worn and appeared to be made in a very fine manner. The deep tones of the brown leather and the lighter colored stitching were elegant.

There were no markings or words on the envelope. He rose from his chair and handed it to me across the large elegant desk.

"Read the contents and then I'll burn it."

The document introduced one Ernesto Cartinega, a revolution-ary living in Costa Rica. He had made himself into a nuisance to the United States and its plans for Central and South America. I was given no details about that situation. My job was to make him disappear. He would be at a certain fishing lodge in Costa Rica from January 14th to the 20th. I had reservations at the lodge—to fish—that same week. The method of his disappearance was my problem. Several weapons would be at my disposal. How they got to be at my disposal was apparently not something I needed to know. I only needed to know where they would be hidden or stored at the lodge. Collateral damage for this mission was okay—no preconditions or limits other than not getting caught and not leaving evidence to associate me with the death/disappearance. "How will I remember these details?" I asked without raising my head from my reading.

"Memory," he said. "And we will give you an itinerary that will help you recall what you read in the packet. You'll be going on a five day fishing trip. Plan the job so you leave before any evidence can be found. We will provide a float plane to bring you in and get you out in a timely fashion."

This was a new approach to killing people. In the military, I had an organization and a team. Here, I had an organization for certain support, but I was mostly, on my own.

"What resources are available to me and how do I contact them?"

"Yes, resources. What resources do you think you might need?"

"I'll need to know where he will be and when he will be there, for example. I'll need to know what contingencies are available to me if things do not work according to plan."

"Good questions and a simple answer. We will always provide you with as much before-hand information and equipment as reasonably possible, but once you leave on a mission, you're on your own. We need complete deniability. If you're caught or your cover is broken, we will not help you. In fact, we may have to kill you ourselves to keep you from getting into the wrong hands. You see, Michael, the United States does not sanction or condone assassinations." A wry smile crossed his face but was fleeting. "Of course, as in most businesses, once someone proves themselves a reliable asset, the initial offering improves dramatically." Again that smile.

I understood what he was telling me. This was to be my test. If I performed well, then there would be benefits. He went into great detail regarding the placement of my weapons cache, and my potential escape routes. I had a boat, a float plane, and even a jeep that could get me to a secondary destination. He gave me what appeared to be a pocket cigar case. It was metallic, appeared to be silver, and contained two very fine Cuban cigars. It also contained a lighter which in addition to lighting my cigars produced a powerful signal to identify my whereabouts should I need alternate means of transportation for my trip home. The signal was activated by turning the screw under the lighter which looked like the cover for the lighter fluid well.

After I read the material several times, Jim tossed it into the fireplace. He handed me an airline ticket out of Newark to San Jose, Costa Rica. The flight would depart on January 12. A float plane would pick me up at the airport in San Jose and fly me to Puntarenas where the fishing lodge was located. I would be fishing in the Golfo de Nicoya. Permit, Tarpon, Sailfish in mid-January. I was thrilled with the fishing trip but understood that it would be a secondary benefit, if at all. This mission had to be perfect if I expected a future in the 'asset' business.

"Now, some additional details," he said after nothing but ash was left of the instruction and information packet. "Here are the lodge pamphlets and pictures. You may select whatever fishing gear you think you need downstairs and pick up some good luggage and some clothing. You will have an account at the store which will be paid by us in full at the end of each month. Use it to outfit yourself for your trips. You'll never need to be concerned about it. It is in your name, but is billed to a company of which you now own a small part. This will be the routing of your payments for travel expenses and your account here. When we no longer have a relationship, these accounts will disappear. You will only make withdrawals, never deposits. We will make the deposits.

The company is called Emerging Medical Devices. It's located in Singapore. They have opened a Swiss Bank Account for you to receive your share of profits. There is a patent for a field kit used in wartime by combat medics. You are the designer of that kit and holder of the patent. This is why you are a wealthy man and able to travel as you do."

He showed me a piece of paper that bore my name and a picture of a pocket-sized kit containing several small stainless instruments that could be used to debride, suture, and probe wounds, and place a tracheotomy. The instruments slipped together so that they were difficult to lose once inside the small case about the size of a passport cover and half an inch thick. It fit easily into the shirt pocket of fatigues, which it was designed to do. The case was made of aluminum, water-tight and air-tight.

He went on, "So, this little instrument packet idea was purchased from you by a British company in Singapore, and in return you have certain benefits and a piece of the pie. The company is privately owned and anyone can check out your association with it. Here is a letter from the company to you, detailing your good fortune and how you shall be paid, periodically. from a share of the profits. It is dated today and you may go ahead and celebrate your good fortune with your wife. However, she may not use the charge account here," he added parenthetically. "And finally, here are several numbers. This card is useless without the code word." He handed me a three by five card upon which was printed marginatus obligatum. "Memorize this now," he said. I looked at it and committed it to memory. He threw the three by five into the fire and added a log from a neat stack in a brick portal beside the hearth.

He gave me the plastic card which looked like a credit card. It had *Abercrombie and Fitch* printed across the top.

"The lower numbers represent a telephone number. You'll use this to do any banking. You will never use any phone accept the payphone here at Abercrombie's on the sixth floor inside the door marked 'private' at the back of the Picture Gallery. This is a phone for special customers. You will only need a quarter to get a dial tone. Thereafter everything is free of charge and the coin is returned when you hang up. You may not transfer any of the funds in your special account to any other account. When you want to withdraw money you will so indicate and you will be sent a check which will reflect profit taking from your share of the company and indicate that taxes have been paid on the draw. It will come to your home address. The numbers above the lower numbers are a code which identifies you to your account manager when used with the password. Do you have any questions about the account?"

"Not at this time," I said.

"Do you have any questions at all?"

Self-reliance was a big part of my new job. It needed to begin now. "Just one," I said, "Do I ever get in touch with you or are we on a one way communication network?"

"If you call that same number on your credit card, but instead of giving your account number, simply use the code word, I'll call you back within a few minutes at the phone on the sixth floor. Never any place else. Remember all calls in or out are only from the phone on the sixth floor. Oh yes, and this," he said, and handed me one of the field surgery kits I had allegedly designed. "The author needs an example of his work," he said and we got on the elevator. This time it went down to the eighth floor where I selected some fishing rods and reels appropriate for saltwater fly fishing, and several pieces of fine luggage appropriate for a physician sportsman.

CIVILIAN LIFE

CIVILIAN LIFE

I returned to the apartment with my new luggage and fishing equipment. Mary Elizabeth was back with our daughter.

"Wow, where did you get all of that?" she said noticing the Abercrombie and Fitch name on the bags and boxes.

"I treated myself to some nice luggage. Going on a fishing trip to Costa Rica in January. I'll only be gone for five days."

"Really," she said. "Did you ask me if I wanted to go?"

"Actually I did not because I don't want you to come."

"What the fuck are you talking about?" She yelled so loudly that Mackenzie, who had been napping, jolted awake and began to cry.

"What is wrong with you?" I said. "I intend to have a life. I have some money that is mine. It is in a trust that you may never have. The trust has strict rules. I can use the money for our benefit, but you may never have access to it other than through my good will. Keep acting like a shit, Mary Elizabeth, and you'll see none of it."

"Fuck you," she said. "You never said anything about a trust."

I showed her the letter I had received. She read it and handed it back to me. "Just how much money are we talking about?"

"It's better you don't know. Just leave it alone."

She stared at me with almond-bitter eyes.

"Look, I'm trying to figure out what I want to do with my life. Being out of the military because of a wound was not expected. So now there are new choices and decisions. Maybe, it will be practicing medicine, travel, fishing and hunting. Maybe we can travel as a family—but not all the time. We each have our own lives and we have the life we share. Isn't that how you want it to be?"

"I don't feel like discussing this now," she said, and walked into the study. She ignored Mackenzie who was still crying.

I turned on the Hi Fi and placed a Neil Diamond record on the turntable. Mackenzie loved Neil Diamond. I picked her up and we danced to *Mr. Bojangles*—one of her favorites. She laughed and rested her little head on my shoulder as we danced around the living room. "Love Dada," she said.

Christmas was in less than two weeks and I'd be off to Costa Rica in less than a month. It was an exciting time, anticipating this new adventure. It got my mind off Mary Elizabeth. We were going to my sister's for Christmas. She and my brother-in-law knew how to give a party. There would be plenty of turkey and ham. My sister's mushroom soup was magnificent and my brother-in-law's holiday punch, superb. Just thinking about the ingredients brought the taste to my palate—gingerale, club soda, pineapple juice, orange juice, rye whiskey and strawberries.

Mary Elizabeth emerged from the room we referred to as the study as I was contemplating Christmas Punch. The study was actually the third bedroom in my co-op apartment. After we were married we bought a second desk for her and reorganized the room so we both could use it. My mind was not as yet adjusted to the apartment being ours; mine and Mary Elizabeth's. It belonged to me and she was living there. After the events of the past several years, I saw her as a manipulative bitch who wormed her way into my life like a cancer invades its host. As much as I tried to love her, she never gave me cause but instead smashed my efforts with incredibly unloving and selfish choices and behavior. In this situation she did not deviate from the pattern.

"Michael me darling," she began after she sat in one of the sitting room chairs. "Ya know how much I love you and the wee little one, but I have to have an equal opportunity life."

"What the hell are you talking about?" I said. "You came after me. I was perfectly happy without you. But then there was the pregnancy and we lost the first baby and now here we are with a one and a half year old daughter. Believe me, I'd have left long ago if you didn't keep getting pregnant."

"Fuck you, you son-of-a-bitch. You had to fuck me for me to get pregnant, didn't you?"

"True, but just think about how many times we have had sex and then consider your pregnancy rate. It must be near one hundred percent, no?"

"So what the fuck does that mean? I can't help being fertile."

"You could be on birth control pills. I could have used a condom, but you completely ignore me romantically and then you strike like a fucking black widow when I'm hurting and vulnerable and wanting so much to be able to love you."

"So are you saying you don't love me, you bastard? Well, I hate you. You've taken everything away from me."

"What?"

"You don't believe in God. You hate my aunts. What do I have left?"

"Mary Elizabeth, my spiritual convictions have nothing to do with yours. Whether or not I like your family is irrelevant to our relationship. I truly love your dad. But I see how the women in your family treat the men. The women seem to suffer from the effects of religion with a pathetic lack of romantic lust for their men. The men become drunkards just to survive life with such women. I'll not be a drunkard and I'll not put up with that kind of shit. I've tried to get you to free your romantic inclinations, but look at how you dealt with my long absence and my being wounded. Did you ever write me a love letter? Did you jump my bones when I returned home? Did you hold me and kiss me tenderly—a long wet lusty kiss?"

"Fuck you, Michael Ross. I'm not that way. You knew it when you married me."

"No, Mary Elizabeth. I left you. Then you came calling. Remember? You told me that terrible story about being raped as a teenager. You captured my compassion and sympathy. Then you seduced me and became pregnant. I never wanted you. I felt sorry for you."

She stood up, put on her coat and scarf and left. As she closed the door behind her the idea that she might never return was looming in my mind. A sinister feeling swept over me. A lifetime with Mary Elizabeth O'Rourke was not in the cards. The idea of it was like the skin-jarring sensation of a mortar round that had landed too close. These morbid ideations were interrupted by the familiar cry Churchill made when Mackenzie was pulling on his hair. He laid there and suffered because he instinctively knew that if he tried to escape when she had a hold of him, he might hurt her. Churchill was a superior dog.

They were in the master bedroom. Mackenzie had taken a nap after our dance. She fell asleep on the floor under Churchill's watchful eye. The manner of his protection was astonishing. When she slept, he never left her side and permitted few people near her. I was one. Mary Elizabeth and my mother were the others. Mary Elizabeth's best friend Eleanor had once tried to lift Mackenzie from her crib and Churchill showed his fangs and a menacing guttural growl.

Now, Mackenzie was awake and embracing him—to her it was embracing—her two little hands full of his hair, pulling as hard as she could while leaning on his head. Churchill's cries were for help. I distracted Mackenzie so she'd let go of him. Then Mackenzie, Churchill and I prepared some dinner for ourselves—Kosher hotdogs and pea soup. We had a pleasant quiet evening.

Mary Elizabeth returned sometime during the night. I only knew this because she was sleeping on her side of the bed when I awoke the next morning. Whenever we had an emotional, angry disagreement, she behaved as if it never happened. So no further mention was made of my forthcoming trip. We spent Christmas with my family at oldest older sister's and Mary Elizabeth performed well, as if we were the happiest young family in the world. There was just one awkward moment when my brother-in-law tried to understand why she wanted to spend time and money studying Elizabeth Bowen and Eudora Welty. "What can come of it?" he said.

"It's intellectually stimulating," she said.

"So are a million other things that have some connection to real life," he said.

"Well, I'm enjoying it," she said.

When my brother-in-law noticed his guests were getting uncomfortable he had backed off. Like me, he never understood Mary Elizabeth.

The week between Christmas and the New Year I visited with Dr. Robinson, the new chief of medicine of the Columbia P&S service at Harlem Hospital Center. He offered me two options, work as an ER attending or there were two fellowships available, one in cardiology the other in hematology. I decided on the ER attending position. It came with a month's vacation, a decent salary, and a faculty appointment—Instructor in Medicine. The Harlem ER was like a warzone. I'd feel at home there. The position opened in February of '71, three, 12 hour shifts per week.

With my medical career on the move, all that was left was to organize my thoughts for the job in Costa Rica. Was it a mission or a job? I wasn't certain. I went to the NY Public Library and studied maps of Costa Rica. I studied charts of Golfo de Nicoya. And later that day, when I took Churchill for his daily run in the park, I brought my fly rod and practiced casting and the double haul, a maneuver necessary to shoot line out far enough to entice a feeding Tarpon or Sailfish. Casting was awkward in a heavy ski jacket with wind and blowing snow, but if I could do it well under these conditions, it would be easy on Golfo de Nicoya.

I made arrangements with my mother to leave Mackenzie Claire and Churchill with her and my dad while I was in Costa Rica.

"Wow, a fishing trip way down there?" My dad said.

"Yes, while I was being treated at Tripler, I met a fellow with loads of money who enjoyed my sense of humor. He travels all over the world. He invited me on this trip. How could I refuse? Besides, I don't start at the hospital until February. It will work out perfectly."

"Lucky you," my mother said, but she had a tone that suggested she didn't believe me. I didn't take the bait.

The flight to San Jose was out of Newark. I planned to drop my daughter and my dog off at my parents' and then park the Monza at the airport.

"No, no," my dad said. "I'll drive you to the airport. Your car will be safe here."

So, I arranged for the Monza to have service and body repairs while I was away. Mary Elizabeth could do without a vehicle for that time.

JUST ANOTHER JOB

JUST ANOTHER JOB

The trip was uneventful. I arrived in Puntarenas on schedule and settled into my room after meeting a Mr. Santoro, who was the owner. My quarters were actually a one room cottage on a beach along the shore of Golfo de Nicoya. It was white stucco with red windows and a red door. Inside was a bed covered with mosquito netting, a few chairs, and a full bath. There was no glass in the window openings, only bamboo blinds and wood shutters to protect against wind and rain when necessary. You could fish with or without guides. Mine was the premium package, so I could do as I pleased. I took a short nap and by late afternoon, felt hungry. The central gathering place was a large thatched-roof open pavilion. The fishing coordinator was seated at a lovely wood desk that must have been eight feet by four feet at least. It faced the center of the pavilion and when a guest stood facing the desk, the topaz blue gulf was the background. The fishing coordinator assigned guides and gave out the day's information including where fish had been seen, the tides, and the sea and weather conditions. Her name was Maria, according to the sign on her desk. The pavilion also housed the dining room where meals were served and a very nicely appointed bar offering the finest beverages and cigars. If a blowing rain came, there were wood shutters that swung down on hinges to give the interior some protection. When they were not down, the shutters acted as awnings of a sort.

About three hundred feet from the pavilion was the Nicoya Fishing Lodge's dockage. The float plane had landed there, and at least a dozen 17 foot flat bottom boats were secured to the dock. The boats were all the same with forty horsepower outboards, a polling platform at the stern, and a casting platform at the bow. They were tied to the dock in 3 orderly rows of 4 to 6, side by side. They all were painted a subdued yellow.

That first afternoon I explored the property as a tourist should, and took pictures with my 35mm Leica. I noted where the flats boats appeared to be fishing. Most, close to shore. Too close for my needs because of the possibility of being seen or heard from the beach.

My weapons cache became a part of my luggage when I was boarding the float plane. It was a leather rod and reel case bearing my name but was not part of my original boarding luggage in Newark. I was impressed with the efficiency of the agency.

In the stucco hut which served as my room, I placed the case with the rest of my fishing gear. I did not attempt to hide it. It had a lock which opened with the same key that opened the case I had purchased at Abercrombie's—nice touch Jim, I thought. Inside, a machete, a Colt forty-five pistol with a silencer, and a Swedish rifle with a 6mm magnum cartridge box containing four rounds were neatly and securely placed. The rifle was disassembled. There was a Leitz scope and silencer for the rifle.

In the pavilion, guests mingled and I met Señor Ernesto Cartinega, a loud, humorous, confident man, built like a professional soccer player. He was taller than I by an inch or two. I thought I could probably defeat him with a knife, but how could I be sure? It was better to never over or under-estimate the enemy. I learned that early on in my military training days. Cartinega spoke excellent English. We struck up a conversation while enjoying some French brandy after the meal, which had been a variety of grilled local fish, roasted plantains, fresh baked bread and some form of cooked seaweed.

"So Hombre, you are from New York?" he inquired as he drew in the smoke of an expensive Cuban cigar.

I was also smoking one. I blew the smoke out of my mouth, savoring the flavor of the cigar and the brandy. "Yes, I live in the City."

"And what do you do to afford these expensive excursions to exotic Central American fishing spots in the middle of winter?"

"I'm a physician," I said.

He laughed long and hard. "So what I hear about American doctors is true then."

"And what is it that you hear?"

"That you are rich fat cats who love the finer things in life."

"All true," I said. "So how is it that you come to be a rich fat cat?" I asked

He looked at me with a menacing stare, but then laughed and said he was in the import export business and had been in many right places at right times.

I raised my brandy glass and said, "Here is to being in right places at right times."

"Yes," he said. "And here is to being in the right woman at the right time."

"I'll drink to that," I said.

"Are you a married man?"

"What is your point?" I asked

Again he laughed loud and long. "I like you Hombre. Why don't we fish together tomorrow?"

"A grand idea Ernesto. Let's go see where the biggest meanest fish are"

We discussed the fishing opportunities for our first day outing with Maria. She was a lovely Costa Rican woman likely in her thirties. She had well tanned skin, a long slender body with breasts large enough to jiggle when she moved. She wore a lose-fitting white dress that exposed plenty of leg and breast and she smelled of some expensive scent. Ernesto had difficulty keeping his eyes off her breasts. I made sure to look her directly in the eye as I spoke with her.

"So gentlemen, do you want to catch sailfish, tarpon, permit?" She paused and smiled, "Or perhaps you might enjoy something a bit more challenging?"

"Such as?" I said.

"Apparently we have an invasion of bull sharks just off the reef at the entrance to the Gulfo de Nicoya. Have you ever caught a bull shark on a fly rod?"

The idea appealed to Ernesto. He nodded his head and slowly blew out a mouth full of smoke. It appealed to me because I could work this into my plan quite successfully.

"What do you think, Hombre? Are you game?" he asked me.

"I'm game as long as we can meet this challenge without an entourage of guides and assistants to dilute the thrill and the danger."

"How about one guide and a 17 foot boat?" Maria asked. She was smiling at Ernesto.

"Perfect," I said.

Ernesto drew thoughtfully on his cigar, looked at me with his dark eyes, blew the smoke out through pursed lips and smiled. "Yes, Hombre, you and I against the bulls, mañana."

"Thomaso is young and strong and knows the sharks," Maria said. "He will make a good guide for the two of you."

"Good, Thomaso it is," Ernesto said.

We returned to our seats on the beach-side of the pavilion where the evening breeze and the sound of small waves rhythmically breaking added to the tropical ambrosia of the place.

"So, shall we put a wager on the largest shark?" Ernesto asked.

"How much of a wager?"

"You tell me," he said.

"How about one hundred dollars for each foot, or part, larger than the next largest caught by the opponent?"

"Done," he said.

I slept well that night. Perhaps it was the sea air, the rhythm of the breaking waves or perhaps the brandy and the excitement of anticipating the kill. I had formulated a plan with numerous variations. When my eyes closed I was confident it would work. It included sharks.

In the morning we boarded a slightly larger boat with a 100 hp outboard. The boat was 22 feet long, but still had the polling platform at the stern and the casting platform at the bow. In my beach hut, I placed the 45 pistol in one of my Abercrombie tackle bags with a chambered round and a full magazine. If anyone discovered it, I'd say it was protection against the sharks. I'd say I always bring it when I fish for large saltwater species.

Thomaso was likely in his twenties and built broadly and low to the ground. He looked like he could bench-press three or four hundred pounds. He loaded my gear and his gear. Ernesto had none of his own. He was already drinking rum and coke and it wasn't yet 9am. He had not been at breakfast in the pavilion, but showed up laughing, still puffing on a large cigar and carrying the rum drink.

"Hombre, do you need some fuel to get your motor started?"

"I'm fueled with caffeine," I said.

He pointed to the large round cooler he was carrying. "Well, whenever your tank needs a refill, you let me know."

Thomaso maneuvered the boat out of its slip and we set off south across the Golfo de Nicoya toward Cabo Blanco. I'd examined charts and it looked like about 15 to 20 nautical miles to reach the location of the sharks, which were near an island on the southeast coast of the Nicoya peninsula. The sea was a magnificent blue and we saw schools of fish just below the surface running from feeding predators. Some may have been bull sharks, others, sailfish, barracuda, or Dorado. The ride was fairly smooth, but wet. My lightweight slicker was keeping me dry from the occasional spray flying onboard due to a light chop and wind generated by the boats speed. Thomaso loaned a slicker to Ernesto, who leaned back against the center console of the boat and continued to drink his rum and smoke his cigar. Actually, the cigar got wet and went out but he held it between his teeth, nonetheless.

Just as the rhythm of the boat's movement and the sea spray were lulling me into a state of relaxation, Thomaso slowed the skiff and studied the surface. Open ocean appeared to our south and east. There was a small island to our northwest, and the shoreline of the Nicoya peninsula beyond it in the distance. He idled the engine and took a foul-smelling rubber bag filled with fish parts and blood from one of the boats storage compartments. Ernesto complained of the stench.

"It smells like a whore's rag," he said and puffed hard on his cigar trying to relight it with his Zippo.

"Fish guts and chicken blood," Thomaso said. "It will bring the sharks." He placed the bag over the side and tied it to one of the skiff's docking cleats.

"Now, Señor Ross, do you have a 12 weight fly rod in that case?"

"No, I have a 10 and an 8 weight."

"Not enough for these monsters," he said. "I'll give you one of mine. Who will fish first?"

"Ernesto," I said. "You first."

"No, no, Hombre. You begin so I can learn what I must do to defeat you." He refilled his rum and coke.

I noticed the first dorsal fin slipping through the azure water about twenty yards from the boat.

"Eiyee," Thomaso shouted, "It must be at least a twelve-footer." He was pointing at the fin that I was following with my eyes. "Get up on the bow platform and do not fall in the water," he said to me.

"Hombre, that fucking shark is twice your size," Ernesto said. He wiped his lips with the sleeve of his slicker then removed it, tossing it to the floor of the skiff. Thomaso picked it up and quickly put it into a locker under his helm seat.

"You must be ready to cast that streamer at the shark when I tell you to do so." He dipped the streamer in a small can of chicken blood and threw it over the side. "Just leave it in the water until I tell you to cast it," he said.

As we waited for the monster to move in closer, I saw a shadow growing out of the depths and rising fast under the foot long streamer tied to my line. The first ten feet of line were made of braided wire so the shark's teeth and rough skin could not easily cut it. I pointed toward my streamer and said, "Thomaso!"

He looked into the water and shouted, "Hold the bow rail, Señor Ross." As the last word rolled off his lips the bull shark rose out of the water. It was eight or ten feet long. I saw the teeth as the mouth opened to devour the streamer sitting about five feet from the boat. The shark cleared the water up to the base of its tail and as it fell back into the sea slammed into the skiff. I held the rail with my left hand and set the hook by bringing the fly rod tip up smartly as soon as the shark was back into the water. The pull on the rod felt like a train. I braced my body against the bow rail and leaned forward, reeling in as I did. But the shark was on the run. He headed toward open water. Thomaso put the engine in gear, pulled the bloody stinking sack into the skiff and began to follow the powerful creature hooked on my line.

"Señor Ross, keep the line taught. Reel in whenever you can and if he jumps, lower the rod tip. I think you have hooked him well."

I fought the shark for about 20 minutes. My arms were weary when Thomaso finally grabbed the leader and pulled the shark alongside the skiff. Meters were marked off along the gunwales of the boat.

"He is nine meters Señor Ross. A fine catch. Do you want a picture?"

Once Thomaso had the leader my eyes were on Ernesto. He was feeling his rum, having some difficulty standing and looking over the side at the shark. Thomaso had placed the blood bag back into the water and there were now at least five other dorsal fins circling the boat.

"Look at this monstor," Ernesto. You might as well pay up now," I shouted.

"No fucking way, Hombre. I'll catch a bigger one. Look at that son-of-a bitch coming to take a chunk out of your shark." He pointed to another bull shark headed like a torpedo at the still hooked shark beside the boat.

Thomaso cut the leader and grabbed for the wheel on the console. Ernesto was between me and the gunwale. When the charging bull shark struck, the boat recoiled and I took advantage of the opportunity to push Ernesto into the water. He was powerful even though drunk but being off balance and tipsy from the rum he went overboard with little effort on my part.

"You stupido. You fucking gringo!" He was shouting as his body went airborne and fell backwards into the attacking bull shark and the exhausted shark Thomaso had just cut loose. The attacking shark sunk its lower jaw into the flank of the exhausted shark. Blood was gushing into the water as Ernesto tried to pull himself back into the boat, but a third shark grabbed his left leg and began thrashing about trying to tear off a mouthful of flesh. Ernesto yelled from the pain but did not let go of the boat.

Thomaso leaned far overboard to get a grip on Ernesto's body and pull him back into the boat. I dropped my fly rod and opened the compartment where my tackle bag was stowed.

"No, no," Thomaso shouted. "Help me pull him into the boat."

But the shark that had a hold on Ernesto was not about to release its prey. We had a feeding frenzy on our hands and the boat's blood bag, the shark that was bleeding from a missing mouthful of flank muscle, and Ernesto were the prime objectives.

"Señor Ross, please help me, I can't hold him."

The decision was a fast one. One of the alternatives I had considered the night before. Although I didn't want Thomaso to be collateral damage, I couldn't chance his surviving to wonder why I had pushed Ernesto overboard. This was a perfect opportunity. I pulled the 45 out of the bag and shot Thomaso in the head. Ernesto was screaming, now. He knew what was about to happen. His eyes flashed at me and he spat as the shark that had him pulled him under. Another shark, perhaps that twelve footer, got Ernesto's head in its mouth and began to writhe and rip at it until it came off. I grabbed Thomaso's feet and held his head under water.

Sharks feeding on one object often do not change to another. It was for this reason I had shot Thomaso—to get his blood flowing, which 45 caliber head wounds do nicely. So it took only a moment for another of the monsters to clamp its jaws on his head. I had my feet braced against the gunwale and held his feet locked in a vice grip with my arms. The shark was tearing and rolling. Another shark, seven or eight feet long, almost jumped into the boat leaving teeth marks on the gunwale and the deck as it tore the blood bag from the rope that held it and nearly capsized the boat. The shark that had a hold on Thomaso's head finally succeeded in decapitating him. It was also a large beast, at least ten feet long.

I put the engine in gear, and held Thomaso's headless body, only pulling it into the skiff once the boat was moving steadily away from the blood clouds and body parts in the water. I was covered with blood and sweat and sea water. Ernesto's body continued to be torn apart by frenzied sharks. The water was clear enough to see the slaughter going on just below the surface. Nothing identifiable was left of Ernesto. Body parts, shreds of clothing, blood and deck shoes covered the surface around the boat and smaller bull sharks, five and six footers, were swallowing up the human debris. Thomaso's head with the forty-five hole in it was no where to be seen, hopefully digesting in a shark's belly. A perfect kill—mission accomplished.

The boat slowly moved further out into the sea, which was calm with gentle shallow swells. After I had gone out of sight of the island and the Nicoya peninsula, I wiped of my prints and tossed the forty-five overboard in what appeared to be very deep darker blue water and watched it sink out of sight.

I poured myself a long cold rum and coke and examined the skiff as my thirst subsided. The headless body of Thomaso and the gashes in the fiberglass from biting sharks' teeth were a grand deception of the truth. Several shark's teeth were embedded in the boat. I pulled one out with a pair of pliers and gripping it with the needle-nosed tool, cut several gashes into the meaty part of my left hand. Then the tooth went into my tackle bag as a memento. "Well done," I muttered to no one in particular and turned the boat back toward the lodge at Puntarenas.

Once in site of the shore I used the small handheld radio hanging from a cord on the console and called out "Mayday, Mayday." After less than five minutes someone answered and I said there had been a shark attack and two men were dead. A boat raced out to meet me as I headed back to the lodge. It was a forty-footer. Ernesto's bodyguard was on board as well as several other men including the lodge owner.

"Oh Sancti Christi," the owner was shouting and repeating as he saw the headless body and the blood.

"Where is Señor Ernesto!" his body guard said looking bewildered by his absence.

"He fell overboard. A huge bull shark attacked the boat while we had a smaller one we had caught pulled alongside. The boat almost went over. Ernesto was attacked as soon as he hit the water. Thomaso tried to grab him and another shark took off his head. When it was over, there was no sign of Ernesto," I said. I spoke with a low disturbed voice, as if I were having a terrible time keeping my wits about me.

The owner jumped into the skiff. "Oh Sancti Christi," he said again, looking at the shark's teeth broken off in the gunwale. "You are lucky to be alive, Señor," he said to me.

They covered Ernesto's corpse with a tarp and tied the skiff up to the larger boat. We did not race back to the lodge. What was the point?

"Are you alright, Señor Doctor Ross?"

"I'm as well as can be expected," I said.

"Here, drink some more of this. It will help to ease your nerves." He poured more of the rum and coke into my glass, which I had already half emptied. Another man was using the contents of the first aid kit to clean and dress the shark bite wound on my left hand.

"Look Mr. Santoro, I don't want or need any trouble. This was the worst thing I've ever experienced. Please, no reporters coming after me. Don't give my name to anyone. At least do this for me," I said, sounding like I was about to lose control of myself.

"I shall honor your request, Señor. But, the police will want to talk to you. I'm sure they will understand your request for anonymity. You do not need to relive this day over and over again."

"Thank you," I said.

"I told him I wanted to go with him," Ernesto's bodyguard said. "I told him but he refused. He said he was on vacation and didn't need me hanging over his shoulder."

"You could have done nothing," I said. "Once he fell into the water the sharks immediately got his head."

"Why did he fall in and you and Thomaso did not?" the bodyguard asked with an accusatory tone.

"He began drinking before he got on board this morning," I said. "That could be why he lost his footing. But that shark attack was powerful and the boat was jolted. I think Thomaso had the wheel to hold himself from going overboard. I held onto the bow rail because I was on the fishing platform. Ernesto was leaning over the side looking at the caught shark. The one that attacked it was even bigger. When he tried to help Ernesto, Thomaso also fell overboard. I was able to grab him, but another shark got him by the head. And yet another tried to take off my hand." I held up my bloody left hand. "Perhaps you need a bigger boat to catch the bull sharks," I said. "It was terrible," I said, and then I lowered my head and pretended to vomit over the side, just spitting out some of the rum and coke.

"Sancti Christi," Mr Santoro said and placed a reassuring hand on my shoulder. "I'm so sorry, Señor Ross. "What can I do to show you how sorry I am," he said. "I will not charge you for your stay here, of course."

"No, no, Mr. Santoro. I wanted to catch the bull sharks and so did Ernesto. We were excited at the idea of it. But are the sharks always as aggressive as they were this morning?"

"I can only tell you we have never had anyone killed like this. Some years ago one of our guides lost a few fingers trying to cut the leader on a hooked shark, but nothing like this. Nothing like this."

I rode the rest of the way back to the lodge in silence, thinking only about my good fortune. Yes......except for Mary Elizabeth O'Rourke, my life was grand.

AND LIFE GOES ON

AND LIFE GOES ON

I stayed one more day in Puntarenas. Mr. Santoro would accept no money and gave me a refund check which included my airfare. "Please consider returning to the lodge when you have healed from this disaster, Señor Ross," he had said.

This was unlikely. For several days Ernesto's bodyguard had Santoro search the area where we had fished looking for any remains. They found a foot inside of a sneaker floating on the surface. The bodyguard identified the sneaker as Ernesto's.

Several weeks later twenty-thousand dollars showed up in my Swiss bank account. I checked from the secure phone in the Abercrombie store. My first withdrawal of 4500 dollars purchased a 1971 Corvette convertible. I gave Mary Elizabeth the fully repaired Monza. Since we rarely needed a car in the city the Corvette would remain in a garage in New Jersey near my parents' home. When I visited them, I usually brought Mackenzie with me. We'd take a bus to Weehawken, walk to the garage I rented for the Corvette, and use the gorgeous metallic-blue convertible to visit Grandma and Grandpa.

In February, as planned, I began working in the ER. A subway or a cab sufficed as transportation to and from the hospital. The income was good and the work challenging. The Harlem ER was always busy and always exciting.

One Saturday evening in March a large black male was brought in by ambulance allegedly unconscious. The medical intern in the ER looked him over and could find no problem other than obvious alcohol intoxication from his breath and the vomit on his shirt both of which reeked of alcohol. The man's wife was with him and she was intoxicated to the point of barely being able to walk. She stumbled around his gurney, mumbling unintelligibly. I asked her if her husband had been drinking or using any other drugs. She muttered something about "fucking street junky" and fell toward the gurney, spitting on the unconscious man. As she did this he rose up and took a round house swing at me. I ducked and his punch hit her squarely in the face, sending several teeth flying to the floor. One of the security guards got the man in a chokehold with his Billy club and another came running over to control his thrashing kicking legs.

The intern asked me, "What the hell got into him?"

"Too much booze, probably some heroin, cocaine and or speed."

"Holy shit," the intern said. "Good thing you ducked, Dr Ross."

"Yes, good thing," I said with a smile I couldn't help because I enjoyed the irony of his punching out his wife's teeth, when I knew he was trying to hit me.

A few hours later, on that same night a teenage boy arrived with a stab wound. He was conscious and stable in spite of the 7 inch knife blade still in place in his neck. The handle extended from the right side of his neck and about an inch and one half of blade from the left side. There was little bleeding. Somehow the knife had passed behind his trachea and in front of his carotid arteries. His eyes were surprisingly quiet. I would have expected terror. I was calling for a surgical resident to come and look at him when another young man swearing that the patient with the knife in his neck was his brother came to the ER information desk. The nurse waved for me to come over.

"Look, man, he's my only brother. I want to see him now, man. Don't be no motherfucker. Just let me see him."

"He has a knife in his neck. Any wrong move and it could cut his arteries or his breathing tube."

"I don't give a shit what he looks like. I just need to see him."

"Okay, come on. We'll go together," I said, and motioned to one of the security guards to come with us.

"Who the fuck is this," the patient's brother asked.

"Henry is a security guard. He needs to be with us."

"Hey you motherfucker, what you lookin at?" he said to Henry.

Henry put his hand on his nightstick.

"Just relax young man, or else I will not allow you to see your brother." I pulled back the curtain surrounding the bed of the patient. As the young man with the knife in his neck saw the man alleging to be his brother, I saw the terror come into his eyes.

His alleged brother lunged at him and I heard the switch blade snap open before I saw it. The young man in the bed pulled the knife from his neck and plunged it into the chest of the attacker just as Henry struck the hand with the switchblade with his nightstick. It happened with such speed I stood there for a moment trying to confirm in my mind I had actually witnessed the scene.

When the patient pulled out the knife he severed his windpipe. Now he was making gurgling sounds and choking. His eyes were wide.

I called for an intubation set and a powerful sedative by injection. He already had an IV in place. I gave him the Valium and morphine and intubated him. The surgical resident arrived and took him to the OR. His attacker was quite dead. The knife had sliced open his heart and cut his aorta according to the coroners report. Just another Saturday evening in the Harlem Hospital ER.

When the story finally unfolded, it turned out the incident had to do with gangs and drugs. The alleged brother was a 'gang brother' apparently trying to finish the job he had started. The young man with the knife in his neck survived and was only charged with dealing drugs. The murder was judged to be self-defense. Both I and Henry testified as to what we observed that Saturday night in our own little war zone. In the future I'd be more cautious about relatives.

My romantic relationship with Mary Elizabeth never improved or even changed. Fortunately for me my Playboy bunny friend, Bonnie Lee Barnes was always horny. We fucked regularly. I'd stop by at her place when I finished at the ER, usually in the morning when Mary Elizabeth was fast asleep or at work. After, I'd pick Mackenzie up from daycare if she was there and head home for a hot shower and a nap. Churchill would babysit Mackenzie while I slept, waking me up with a bark if she was getting into trouble. But Mackenzie rarely got into trouble.

Churchill played with her, retrieving a ball she would throw for him, or playing tug-o-war with an old red sock. All of this activity took place in her room. Sometimes she fell asleep in a three foot square box I built for her. It had a porthole for entry and exit. Churchill stood guard at the entrance when Mackenzie was sleeping inside. Basically, the three of us did very well together. Add my parents to the mix and life was perfect. They were always willing to keep Mackenzie if I had to work or travel. Perhaps it was okay with Mary Elizabeth that she was not needed. Perhaps she didn't really care. Mary Elizabeth was all about appearances and need. She needed to be seen as earth-mother and scholar.

The shark-attack incident that took place in Costa Rica never made any news broadcast. This was fortunate. Perhaps the Agency had encouraged the silence. I openly admitted to Mary Elizabeth, my parents and some close friends that there had been a terrible incident with sharks which was why the trip had ended early. I even showed off the scars on my left hand where shark teeth had cut me several times. The tooth I pulled from the boat's gunwale had been mounted and hung from a silver chain which I wore from time to time around my neck.

My beeper worked perfectly to cover medical call. The hospital appeared satisfied with my work in the ER. A good friend named Carl, who had been with me in residency training and now was an attending in private practice used to tell the interns and residents that if they drew a shift with me, they would be well taught and completely safe because I could neutralize dangerous intruders as effectively as I practiced emergency medicine. Most of my colleagues knew of my military career and my combat experience.

And this is how life went for us, Mackenzie, Mary Elizabeth, Churchill and me. Mary Elizabeth continued her graduate education, I earned good money as a physician, Mackenzie spent many hours with me and Churchill, and with my parents. She did not seem to mind the little time spent with her mother. But Mary

Elizabeth was a clever mother. She kept journals about Mackenzie's actions and words, and about her interactions with Churchill. These might someday verify her committed motherhood. That summer of '71, we spent a week in a cabin on Lake Champlain in the Adirondacks. I rented a speed boat, fished for bass and pike and took Mary Elizabeth's father, who joined us, for long boat rides up the lake. The cabin was just north of Chazy Landing. David insisted on paying for the Chris Craft I rented. In the evenings he and I would sit out on the screen porch and drink. David could no longer hold his liquor so I often had to help him to bed. In the morning he would cook breakfast, Mary Elizabeth would sleep until noon and Mackenzie and I and Churchill would go to the private beach behind our cabin. Sometimes David would join us and sit in his beach chair chain smoking Pall Mall cigarettes.

He died the following fall of a massive stroke. The tobacco and alcohol hadn't helped. He left his estate to me. He had told me this was his plan because he felt Mary Elizabeth would mishandle his money. He wanted most of it to go into trust for Mackenzie.

Mary Elizabeth wasn't happy about this arrangement when her father's estate was probated. She nagged me daily about how unfair it was that she had no control over any of her father's money.

"I didn't write his will," I said.

"Fuck you, you bastard," she said.

David O'Rourke thought his daughter was an unreliable pain in the ass. I'd like to believe he trusted me and admired my unwillingness to accept domination by a woman. He told me he respected my service to my country and my infrequent use of alcohol despite having to live with his daughter. "Just don't leave her," he had said.

I paid for David's funeral and had him laid to rest beside his wife and my first born daughter in that Pennsylvania cemetery. I placed close to 450,000 dollars in trust to Mackenzie with myself as trustee. Fuck Mary Elizabeth.

Another year passed. Mary Elizabeth and I continued to drift apart. But as long as I accompanied her to various family and social functions and was socially conversant, she seemed satisfied. She concentrated on her graduate school, now at Fordham University and I on Mackenzie and my work at the hospital. My parents continued to be Mackenzie's primary sitters and I spent a lot of free time driving her around in the Corvette and visiting old friends. I ate as many meals with parents and friends as I did at my apartment. Churchill remained a wonderful companion for Mackenzie. They could play together for several hours and then Mackenzie would fall asleep and nap for another hour or two.

Mostly I remained in the apartment with them, but now and again, I'd go out to test Churchill's abilities. At first it was only down the steps to the first floor, but then I'd run around the block, and finally I even tried to food-shop and return in under an hour.

They were always just fine in Mackenzie's room. Churchill was a dependable sitter and protector for Mackenzie. If she cried he licked her face and brought her his toys. There might have been minor risk in this, but life is filled with more than minor risk. Churchill was more trustworthy than some stranger I might pay to babysit. Although, I did occasionally, employ a nurse from the hospital to babysit Mackenzie, particularly when Mary Elizabeth and I went to the theater or the symphony. It was easier to pick up Michele Donnelly and take her home, than to travel to NJ to drop off and pick up Mackenzie at my parents. There were other benefits in it for me. Michele was only five two but she was perfectly put together and very pretty. She looked like Shirley Temple in her twenties. She loved to suck on my dick and fuck. Her small stature definitely enabled fucking in small spaces. I could sit in the passenger seat of the Monza and she would sit on my lap. Michele Donnelly made evenings out with Mary Elizabeth something very special.

ANOTHER MISSION –
ANOTHER DAY,
ANOTHER DOLLAR

ANOTHER MISSION – ANOTHER DAY, ANOTHER DOLLAR

In December of '71 the Agency contacted me, again. Almost a year had gone by since my last mission. I took a taxi to Abercrombies, called the designated number and Jim called me back.

"How about a visit to Abercrombie's on Saturday? I've got a great trip planned for you. Will noon work?"

"See you then," I said.

Mary Elizabeth took Mackenzie for the day. They were going to visit some of her family in Pennsylvania. I fed Churchill and took him for a good long walk in the Park. Then I took a train to 50th and Madison and walked the five blocks to the store. The elevator to the sixth floor bookstore where Jim wanted me to meet him was a fast ride. A book about bird hunting in Patagonia had my interest when Jim arrived beside me in his usual silent fashion, seeming to materialize out of thin air.

"Yes, a wonderful place to hunt birds, and fish for that matter," he said. "Come on, let's go to the office."

We walked back to the private elevator and rode up to the same wood-lined office. The elevator did not note a floor, just a zero on the panel lit up. Perhaps for office. It felt like we were going up. When the elevator door was fully open, he motioned for me to sit in the same chair and handed me an envelope he had taken from his brief case—the well aged leather one. The envelope was thicker than the last one.

"We were very impressed with your last trip. Nicely done, with a minimum of collateral issues. This one will be equally interesting but perhaps a bit more difficult. After offering me a grand Cuban cigar, which he snipped and lit for me, he left.

I read through the documents. The job was in Florida. I was to go fishing in the Everglades and befriend a fellow who was visiting from Poland, one Novak Wojinoska. He would be down there on a fishing vacation in February. We would stay at the same hotel. Apparently he needed to be removed because he was considered a major threat to the success of a US covert operation in Eastern Europe. And this was all I needed to know for there was no other information about the target. There was a footnote, however, that it would be best if I could do the job so his body was never found, as I had done with Cartinega.

A detailed breakdown of his itinerary was included along with pictures of the Everglades City Rod and Gun Club—the hotel where we would be staying—layout maps of Everglades City and environs plus nautical charts and maps of the Everglades. Once again, I would be the traveling adventuring physician. On this trip, as with the last, I'd be outfitted by the store and additional necessary tools would be found in the trunk of my rental car which I'd pick up at the airport in Miami. A clean-up crew would be available but only if absolutely necessary. The preferred method was for me to accomplish the task, solo. I had two months to prepare.

After about thirty minutes, Jim returned. "Anything else you need to know?"

"Have you ever been fishing in the Everglades?" I said.

"No, but Harry has and he says it's magnificent, a saltwater fly fishing paradise. Best way to do it is out of a flat bottom boat, fifteen to eighteen feet long. You won't be able to involve anyone else here. No collateral damage. This is the part that makes this mission so difficult. Of course we intend to pay you double the money for the successful completion of such a task," he said.

I nodded. "Getting me there several days before Mr. Wojinoska arrives is a good idea. I'll be able to use that time profitably."

"Good. Then let's go down and get you outfitted for the trip."

We spent several hours in the fishing department and the clothing department. Most of the items were shipped to my apartment. I took home an 8 weight and a 12 weight Abercrombie rod and reel, a pair of saltwater wading boots, and a box of saltwater artificials selected by Harry.

We did Christmas at my sister's, again. Mackenzie was the big hit. She was now two and a half, spoke in complex sentences and made jokes. She was a clever child. She loved me and she loved Churchill. She loved my parents, and I suppose she loved her mother, even though Mary Elizabeth did not act like she truly loved Mackenzie. It struck me that she dealt with Mackenzie as she dealt with me. She needed someone to fulfill the husband role of her expectations—that would be me. She needed someone to fulfill the child role to support her needed image of motherhood.

The four of us spent a quiet New Year's Eve in our apartment. I poured some champagne into Churchill's dog bowl, the rest into two glasses and shared a sip with Mackenzie at midnight. We toasted the New Year, 1972, and I tried for the last time to get some kind of warmth and romance out of Mary Elizabeth.

"Can we start this new year with a different perspective?" I said.

"And what might that be?" She asked. "Are you going to start acting like a father and husband?"

"What the hell does that mean?"

"Well, you live life on your own. You work, you spend time with the dog and the child, and you travel. Where do I fit into your plans?"

"Where would you like to fit?"

"Well, I don't know, but it seems like something is missing."

"It is. It's called romance and passion."

"Why does it always come back to sex? I am who I am. I will never change. You need to be satisfied with that. I'm an interesting person. I take care of our home. I've given you a wonderful daughter. What else do you want from me?"

"Passion and romance. I can't live without that and I don't think most normal human males can."

"Well then, I don't know what to say."

"That's it? That's the end of this conversation? You cannot or will not change and I should be grateful for you as you are?"

"Fuck you," she said and left the apartment.

Where did she go when she left the apartment? I looked out the window and watched as she got into the Monza and drove away. If some misfortune befell her, so be it. It was New Years Eve in the City. Downtown would be mobbed because of Times Square. Perhaps she would cross the bridge into NJ and visit with her friend Eleanor. Maybe they'd have girl sex. I also decided to begin a log of Mary Elizabeth's exits from the apartment.

I went into Mackenzie's room and sat in the rocking chair next to her crib and smiled at her peaceful sleeping countenance. Churchill was curled up between the crib and the rocker. His slow easy breathing did not change when I entered the room, nor was any movement apparent until he slid over just a bit to place his head on my foot. I fell asleep in the rocker and dreamed about fishing the Everglades and having sex with beautiful women.

Mary Elizabeth returned around eight in the morning. She brought bagels and Nova.

"Happy New Year to all," she sang in soprano as if the conversation of the night before and her departure had not happened.

I didn't ask where she had been. I didn't care. A receipt from the bakery that was in the same town in New Jersey where Eleanor lived had fallen on the floor by the coat tree. We sat at our 3X4 butcher-block table and enjoyed the good food. Mackenzie loved bagels and Nova as much as her parents.

EVERGLADES CITY

EVERGLADES CITY

I dropped Mackenzie off at my parents' home and took a taxi to Newark Airport. The Eastern flight took me to Miami and a waiting rental car. I have no idea how the CIA managed it, but the reservation was made in my name and a black Abercrombie canvas bag was in the trunk of the car. I did not check the contents at the car rental, but noted the bag when I placed my other Abercrombie luggage into the trunk. The car was a '72 Mustang fastback. It was black. The directions said west on 41 and then south on 29 to Everglades City. I arrived at about 4:15pm on Friday the 25th.

The hotel was in an ownership transition. Nonetheless, service was perfect and the ambiance beyond my expectations. There was a montage of finely finished well aged wood from the lobby to the bar to the billiard room. Walls, floors, cabinets, all wood and plenty of interesting memorabilia displayed on those walls and in glass enclosed tables and cabinets. A stuffed Alligator skin was on the wall in the billiard room. Pictures of notables with their parties and catches were everywhere. Outside, the building was mostly white wood siding with an enormous columned porch wrapped around a good portion of it.

My room was comfortable. It was screened and air conditioned. Full-sized inside shutters allowed for shade from the hot afternoon sun. My bed was a double. The room had that lovely blended aroma of the sea and mildew accompanied by the scent of fresh bed linens and wood polish. A bellhop carried in my luggage, except for the new bag from the trunk of the Mustang which I carried myself. I tipped him and locked the door behind him.

It was time to inspect the contents of the mystery bag. Half inch rope, a very small anchor and chain, a Bowie knife, a sawed-off 12 gauge shotgun, a 9mm German Luger pistol with silencer and a custom built 7mm magnum scoped rifle broken down into four pieces with silencer, everything neatly packed into fitted cases. Serial numbers had been removed from the Luger, shotgun and rifle. According to my instructions, the bag and its contents were to be returned with the car—left in the trunk.

I spent the next two days, Saturday and Sunday, exploring the Cheveleir Bay on the western side of the Everglades. The briefing said this was where my target would likely be fishing. He was apparently quite good at it and would be alone. The waterways were easily negotiated using charts and the compass on the boat I rented, an 18 foot flat bottom with a generous beam and a 40 horse Johnson motor.

Cheveleir Bay contained plenty of fish including some six to eight foot bull sharks and many alligators of similar length. I found several excellent fishing spots and caught two fine snook and a 48 inch black tip shark on my 9 weight fly rod. I released the snook, but brought the shark in with me and left it with a taxidermist to be mounted. Black tip sharks were sleek and powerful. They were superior game fish for a fly rod fisherman and a four-footer was a trophy. After I left the taxidermy shop, I passed a small gift shop and saw half of a 'gators lower jaw bone in the window. I bought it.

Wojinoska arrived late Sunday evening, but he wasn't alone. He had a lovely young woman with him. She was probably in her twenties. The way he fondled her ass-end while checking in suggested she was not a relative, unless, she was a very young wife. According to my briefing, he was in his fifties. He looked older. He was smoking a cigarette while he signed the guest ledger and the smoke kept drifting into his eyes so that he squinted and blinked. His facial skin suggested he had had too much sun and too much nicotine in his lifetime.

I watched from the bar. After registering he walked to the bar with his young female companion. Besides the bartender, the only other person in the bar was me. He and the girl sat at a small table and Wojinoska ordered a bottle of champagne. I told the bartender I'd pay for it. He brought the bottle and two glasses to the table and indicated I had paid for the champagne.

"Oh, no my friend," he called across the room to me, "no need for you to do this." Wojinoska had a thick east European accent.

"You look tired and over-traveled," I said. "Please, allow me the pleasure."

The girl smiled at me in a seductive inviting manner that said she might be for hire.

Wojinoska asked me to join them, but I begged off, saying I had an early busy day of fishing.

"Do you know these waters?" he asked.

"I've spent the last few days exploring Chevelier Bay," I said.

"Is it the usual mangrove islands and inlets?"

"Yes, but with more open water than most of the swamp as far as I can tell."

Now and again he would speak to the girl in what I assumed was Polish and she would smile, sometimes looking at me and sometimes looking down at the tabletop. "I have read much about these waters," he said. "But perhaps you would be willing to show me some of the good spots you have located? It might be fun, no?"

"Of course, but we would need to go in separate boats, if you don't mind. I like my solitude," I said.

"For sure. Separate boats. Besides, I want to take my little flower here with me so I can enjoy her youthful company." He embraced the girl and I saw his hand caress her left breast. She laughed and did not attempt to pull away. She smiled at me as if it was an invitation. He did not see the smile because his lips were on her neck and he was looking down at her full breasts as he caressed the left one and raised it up so it almost slipped out of her low-cut dress. She was not wearing a bra.

"See you at breakfast?" I asked. "I'll be in the dining room around seven."

"Yes, around seven. We look forward to it," he said.

It turned out his room was next to mine. Her laughter placed them in the hall about an hour later. Shortly after that the sounds of their fucking passed easily through the wood paneled walls. I enjoyed the music of her passion. She sang in alto, and the idea that I might get to fuck her crossed my mind.

We met in the dining room just after seven and shared a table for breakfast. Her full face reminded me of a young Kim Novak— her role in the movie *Picnic*. I never heard the girl speak English.

"I'll rent a boat and follow you out to the Bay," he said.

This would fit perfectly into my plans. "Why not rent from the same place where I did?" I suggested.

"Lead the way, my friend. Lead the way."

While he took care of the paper work, she took off her shorts and shirt. I gave her a hand as she climbed down the dock ladder and boarded the 18 foot john boat he had rented. She was wearing a red bikini that displayed her young body. She was lovely to look at and I had to work at turning away.

Once we were on the water, I brought them to several of the better fishing holes located during the preceding days, but never placed myself more than a few miles from where I had left them. He apparently caught a boat-load of snook. As the day progressed, I came by for a visit as if I had run upon them by accident. She was sunning herself, topless. She was not shy and waved to me, her perfect young breasts jiggling as her arm and hand hailed me. He held up a stringer of now mostly dead fish. He was fishing with a spinning rod and reel. "What do you do with all of these?" he asked me.

"I release them after I get them to the boat," I said as my boat pulled up alongside theirs.

He did not seem to mind my occasional look at her naked upper half and her very skimpy bikini bottom. "You want to fuck her?" he asked quite matter-of-factly. "She loves to fuck. She's a high class whore I hired in Warsaw and brought with me. She says she would like to suck your cock." He laughed. The girl looked at me and laughed.

I wasn't sure how to handle the offering. An idea had been coming together in my mind and I had to focus on the mission.

"How about I show you a great place to wade for some very large mangrove snapper? They fight like hell. We'll beach your boat so Beauty can sunbathe. After you're settled into the spot, I'll come back for that blow job." She looked at me and her expression said she understood.

"Sounds like a good plan," he said. He laughed hard and grabbed more than a handful of the girl's right breast. "Maybe we can have her together?" he said, looking for my reaction.

"Maybe later," I said. And he laughed again and said something to the girl in Polish. She looked at me and ran her tongue back and forth across her upper lip.

"Follow me," I said after he had his anchor in the boat.

There was a small beach a few miles away, just large enough to pull the bow of a flat-bottomed eighteen footer onto it. And adjacent to it, but out of sight of the beach was a mangrove island where the mangrove snapper population was abundant. We motored wide open to that beach and pulled their boat halfway onto the sand and then Wojinoska got into my boat. The girl placed a towel on the sand and slipped out of her bikini bottom as Wojinoska and I slowly motored away. I went to the far side of the mangrove island and then came back at idle speed to the gap between the island with the small beach and the mangrove island. The gap was about a hundred feet wide and we were probably 1000 yards from where we had left the young woman. The thick subtropical vegetation on the island with the beach easily kept us out of sight and sound.

"Can I wade here?" he asked me.

"Just let me get you a little closer to those mangroves." I pointed straight ahead. "And make sure you watch for the alligators," I said. "See, there's one right up inside that notch in the mangroves. See it? They're not dangerous as long as you don't corner them and they have not laid eggs."

"I do not see it," he said.

"Look at those two little knobs sticking up out of the water about twenty feet into the notch. See?"

As he strained to look, I struck him hard in the back of the head with the teeth side of the 'gator's jaw bone I had purchased specifically for this purpose. The blow was powerful enough to fracture his skull and knock him unconscious. If someone ever got to examine that skull, it would appear the damage had been done by a 'gator. I tied him with the half inch rope so he could not use his arms or legs and dumped him over the side, holding his body below water for at least ten minutes with one of the oars supplied in case the outboard engine failed. Several other boats passed by at some distance but no one came into the cut because according to the charts it was too shallow. I paddled slowly toward the sunning alligator up in the notch dragging the dead body alongside the boat. Wojinoska's head wound was bleeding heavily. Once the 'gator smelled blood it should take the meal. The oar also worked well to push the dead body further into the notch. A slip knot held the body to the rope and anchor. The 'gator began moving toward Wojinoska, seeming to walk on the bottom and propel itself with its tail. I backed away quickly just as it grabbed his body and began the tear and role move common to alligators and crocs. He pulled the body down and I watched it disappear into the mangrove roots. A good jerk on the rope should remove the anchor and the rope from Wojinoska's body.

We began a tug-o-war, I pulled, the 'gator pulled back. The fight over the body went on for about ten minutes and then the end of the rope and anchor appeared under my boat. I had read about alligator feeding habits and knew they often pulled their quarry into mangrove roots where it would rot and they and the crabs and many small fish would eat at it until poor Wojinoska was no more. Apparently this is what the gators did with one of their primary food sources in the swamp, the nutria, a dog-sized rodent invasive species from South America.

Now it was time to return to the beach where the woman lay naked on her towel. I beached my boat and walked toward her. She sat up. The idea of killing her was not easy for me to accept. She was young, innocent and beautiful and I was one of those males who couldn't turn down the offer of a desirable woman.

"You're getting too much sun," I said.

She smiled but did not understand me. I pointed to the redness on her breasts and arms. "Too much sun," I repeated and held up a tube of suntan lotion. "Let me rub this on you." Some was already in my hands and she smiled at me.

The lotion went on easily over every inch of her. When I arrived at her pussy there was no need for suntan lotion. She spread her legs willingly and I knew what to do—that certain area—she moaned and had an orgasm. Then she gave me a magnificent blow job, slow and deliberate and soft. She continued to moan as if she were savoring some extraordinary food. When she was finished, she swallowed and the idea of fucking her was compelling. My arms wrapped around her and she slid up and closer to me expecting my cock to rise again and enter her. I kissed her hard, her eyes were closed. My eyes scanned the open water of the Bay to insure there were no eyes on us. Her neck broke easily like a tooth pick or a thin branch. She was smiling and her eyes remained closed—a quick good death.

I placed her into their boat and pushed it off the sand. Their anchor line made a good tow rope. Whatever might be found later needed to give the appearance of an accident, or perhaps even that she had been the assassin. Contingency plans were essential. I motored back to the cut by the mangrove island, wrapped their anchor line around her leg and dumped her body into the water—her death should look accidental. Several bull sharks were already swimming about with some urgency, no doubt smelling Wojinoska's blood.

She had no fat on her and sank to the bottom with the anchor. The sharks came in quickly and the small boat was tearing around chaotically. Since I would acknowledge spending some time with them, it did not matter if I left any prints. The part of me left in her stomach could be mine or his, if anything was left of her after the sharks finished. I felt badly that I had never asked her name. But in the end it was all for the best.

When I got back to the inn, I called the desk to inquire if Wojinoska had made a reservation for dinner. He had not, so I made one for the three of us at eight, thanked the person on the phone and showered. Slacks and a sport shirt were appropriate attire for dinner. By nine pm it was getting dark, I was on my third Beefeater martini and they still had not arrived. I walked to the desk and asked if they had returned from their day of fishing. My demeanor was concern but short of panic.

"No Dr. Ross, they have not returned. Maybe they are eating somewhere else tonight. We will be sure to keep an eye out for them."

I returned to my table and ordered a salad and the evening special of grilled fresh grouper. Wojinoska and the girl never showed up. I stopped at the desk again around eleven to inquire if the night manager had heard from them. When he said he hadn't, I urged him to contact the police.

Next morning the search began, but nothing was found. I told the local marine policeman, I had seen them twice during the afternoon and guided them to a fine fishing hole, which I pointed out on my marine chart. My fingertip rested on the chart about twenty miles from the cut containing the alligator and whatever was left of Wojinoska's corpse and the girl's. "He was fishing and she sunning the last time I saw them. It was probably around two or three," I said, and that we talked about the fishing and that the girl needed to be careful of the sun. "I warned them about alligators and the bull sharks because Wojinoska was wade-fishing at the time."

I spent the rest of the week fishing and stayed a good distance north of the mangrove island and that beach. On Thursday the marine police found the empty boat with some of Wojinoska's gear and the girl's blouse. The anchor line was attached to the boat but the working end had been chewed and there was no anchor attached. There were no bodies, blood or body parts found. They found the boat almost ten miles from the mangrove cut. After the bull sharks finished pulling it about as they fed on the girl's body, the usual prevailing wind on the bay and current had done its job—blowing the boat north and west toward the point where I said I had last seen them. Good plans usually pan out.

I caught another magnificent black tip shark on Friday, but I released it. I drove back to Miami on Saturday. Just after I returned the rental car, a tall man in coveralls removed the black bag from the trunk. He got into a van and drove off. The rental car people seemed to ignore him, as if they didn't care or even notice. I took the shuttle to the airport, and flew back to Newark.

Mary Elizabeth actually picked me up at the airport. We drove to my parents and had dinner. I fell asleep in the Monza on the way back to the city and slept soundly. So did Mackenzie. I was forty-thousand dollars richer than I had been a week earlier and reasonably certain there would be more calls from Jim because I was good at my job—imaginative and thorough.

LOOKING FOR PURPOSE

LOOKING FOR PURPOSE

I sold the Monza convertible and bought Mary Elizabeth a Saab. It was safe, durable, and small enough to park easily in the city. It was a golden beige color and she loved it. The transmission was automatic, which she preferred to the four on the floor in the Monza and it wasn't a convertible which also pleased her.

Although I wanted things to work out between us, more for Mackenzie than myself, I couldn't see how they ever would, so, I continued to see my lovely Playboy Bunny at least once a week. She had no expectations except for the fun we had fucking. I made it clear to her that I was married and had no intention of leaving my wife and daughter. She seemed fine with this. Good fortune shined on me in so many ways. Bonnie's willingness to play with me was keeping me sane.

I worked three 12 hour shifts a week in the emergency room. I went to teaching conferences at least once a year to keep abreast of medical science. I liked San Francisco and Chicago. A conference was coming up in Chicago, and I was hoping Mary Elizabeth and Mackenzie might join me.

"What am I supposed to do all day while you're learning to be a smarter physician, play babysitter? I have better things to do," Mary Elizabeth said.

"Such as?" I asked.

"I have books to read. If I go to Chicago, I want to visit their art museum and maybe a play. I don't want to be chasing Mackenzie all over the town. No, you go to your conference and I'll stay right here. Will your parents take Mackenzie while you're away?"

"I'm sure they will, unless they have other plans."

"Well call them. You can't go to Chicago if they can't manage Mackenzie."

As usual my parents were thrilled at the opportunity.

I had a fine conference and Mary Elizabeth did whatever she enjoyed doing in my absence. I invited Bonnie Lee Barnes to join me for a few days in Chicago. She loved the idea. We fucked like rabbits and I didn't even miss any significant teaching sessions. Bonnie returned to New York the day before I left Chicago. On the return flight to Newark I was reading an article in a Chicago newspaper about a man who had attempted to murder his wife, but botched the job and got caught. The wife was in a coma at Cook County Hospital and the husband awaiting trial for attempted murder. I was thinking that if I wanted to kill Mary Elizabeth, I would know how to do the job and get away with it. But I also wondered how I could ever face Mackenzie if I did such a thing. I wasn't sure I had that kind of coldness in me. But then I thought, perhaps I did. What had made me become the man I was? What were my expectations of life and love? What had happened to the romantic in me, the young man who adored Lovey Cohen? But when the stewardess announced we were beginning our approach into Newark, all of these thoughts vanished from my consciousness.

My dad picked me up at the airport. It was a lovely April Saturday, so I walked to the garage I rented for the Corvette, and Mackenzie and I rode up into the Ramapo Mountains. We visited some trout streams and took a few short walks on hiking trails I knew. After, I drove into the city and dropped Mackenzie off at the apartment. Mary Elizabeth had Eleanor over. She apparently stayed a few nights while I was away.

"Eleanor, how nice to see you again."

"I'll bet," she said with a sarcastic note.

"I hope you ladies had a nice respite."

"Why not quit the small talk, Michael, and get that car back to New Jersey. Eleanor and I have plans for tonight and you need to spend some time with your daughter," Mary Elizabeth said.

Churchill was lethargic. He generally became so when Mary Elizabeth took care of him. She did not exercise him enough. "We'll go to the park when I get back, old boy." His tail thumped hard on the floor.

I drove the Corvette back to Jersey and took a bus and a subway train home. By the time I got back, Eleanor had left and Mary Elizabeth was sitting in the living room reading and twirling her hair around her left thumb and index finger, a nervous habit I did not like.

"So, did you and Eleanor have fun while I was in Chicago?"

"We studied. Big tests this week. I'll be gone for most of the week, so don't count on me."

"Where are you going?"

"You know what I mean. I'm going to Eleanor's tonight and I'll be at school and studying in the library most of the week."

"Columbia Library, or NY Public Library on Fifth?"

"What do you care?"

"I really don't care a shit. I was just trying to be interested."

"Fuck you," she said and went into the room we used as our library and reading room. She closed the door. I could hear her speaking to someone on the telephone. I was playing with Mackenzie when I heard her leave. She said nothing to me, just walked out. It was never going to work with us—never.

She did not come home that night or the next and never called me, which was not necessarily unusual. I read the paper, made breakfast for Mackenzie and myself. I didn't know where or how to reach Mary Elizabeth, and she hadn't mentioned anything about Mackenzie during her examination week. She also hadn't left me a note. So I called Mrs. Floric who lived on the first floor and asked her if she wouldn't mind watching Mackenzie until Mary Elizabeth returned from school that night. Mrs. Floric was a woman in her sixties who had lost her husband to cancer a few years before. She had been a staff writer for the NY Times for many years and then had raised two boys of her own. One was a lawyer and the other a NY City police detective. Like most mothers of males, Mrs. Floric loved little girls. She did not yet have any grandchildren of her own, so she enjoyed an occasional visit with Mackenzie. Churchill was a good judge of character, so his lack of enthusiasm for Mrs. Floric definitely affected my willingness to ask her to help out too often.

She came over at five-thirty and I left for the ER. Mary Elizabeth called me at the hospital around eight that evening.

"I'm sorry, I forgot to leave you a note," she said.

"Well, fortunately Mrs. Floric was available."

"Are you working tomorrow?"

"No. I have tomorrow off, but then I have to work Thursday and Friday."

"Okay. That should work out. Once exams are over on Thursday, I thought Mackenzie and I might go out to Eleanor's parents' house in the Hamptons for a few days of rest. Would you mind?"

I knew that if I said I minded she would fly into a tantrum, so I did. "Shit, I thought we might spend some quality time together as a family this weekend," I said.

There was a long pause on the other end.

"Hello, are you sill there?" I asked.

"Of course I'm still here," she said. "Why do you always have to ruin my opportunities to find some peace and happiness?"

"Do I really do that, Mary Elizabeth? Maybe you did it when you seduced me so I'd marry you. Maybe you just have your own fucked-up self to blame."

She hung up. I hated her more every day.

She took Mackenzie to the Hamptons and I spent my time off reading, playing ball in the Park with Churchill, and fucking Bonnie the Bunny. I even took Bonnie out to dinner at my wonderful French restaurant where I never went with Mary Elizabeth. Yes, I took her to Lafayette. We ate magnificent Nuvelle cuisine and drank a fine bottle of Gevrey-Chambertin. After, we returned to her apartment and I fucked her in every orifice. It was a grand evening. I did not mind living a life without Mary Elizabeth. In the taxi on the way back to my co-op, I imagined how delightful it would be, just me, Mackenzie, and Churchill. But there would likely be no such good fortune. I was not about to divorce Mary Elizabeth and allow her to pick my pockets for a lifetime. No, that was never going to happen. I would hang around and make her as miserable as she made me.

She and Mackenzie returned on Monday and I worked my usual 12 hour shift at the ER. Mary Elizabeth returned to classes the following week. We spoke infrequently and were mostly cordial when we did. I had the impression that as long as I continued to provide the life she expected, she would just allow things to ride.

Every day, I reconsidered the just-hang-around-and-make-her-miserable idea. Could I do it? Did I need anything I didn't already have? Perhaps not, but Mary Elizabeth took my life in a direction I had not anticipated. I kept asking myself how and why a girl who hates sex, a girl who was raped as a teen, seduces a romantic womanizer. But then I grappled with the idea of being a womanizer. That had not been my plan. I wanted to meet a wonderful, sexy, adorable girl and love her forever. That had been my original plan. Had I found that girl and passed her by? I knew it wasn't Mary Elizabeth. I wanted to believe that I became a womanizer because of Mary Elizabeth. But, I wasn't ever sure of that. I wasn't even sure I hated Mary Elizabeth, because there were times when I didn't. Nonetheless, something was seriously absent from my life.

AMAZING GRACE

AMAZING GRACE

One early fall day, while walking in Central Park with Churchill and Mackenzie, I realized what was missing from my life. I was soaking in Autumn; the fallen leaves, their scent and colors, the change in light, when the idea blasted me like a brain freeze. There was insufficient grace in my life. I had money and enjoyable, exciting adventures. I had a lovely little daughter and a wonderful dog. Two honorable professions were mine. But there was no romantic love. I fucked many lovely women, but tender, romantic love was missing. Maybe it didn't really exist. I sat on a bench under a tree without leaves. Churchill was looking at a squirrel and Mackenzie had fallen asleep in her stroller, which was too small for her.

The kind of love I had always imagined brought with it, grace. Mary Elizabeth brought with her, anger, self-pity, and disillusionment. These qualities neutralized all grace. Now, I rarely ever imagined romantic love, as if it had been erased from my mind. And grace, where did that idea come from?

About a week after my park-bench epiphany, Mary Elizabeth told me she wanted to study in Europe. She wanted to know if I could manage Mackenzie or if she needed to make arrangements to take our daughter with her.

"I'm going to England. I have an opportunity to study at Oxford. Isn't that wonderful?"

"Oh yes, it's a fantastic opportunity," I said. "Did you get a scholarship or an assistantship?"

"Oh no my dear, you are going to pay for this. After all, I ask for so little."

"Of course, and you also give so little."

"Look you bastard, this is not going to be an argument. You said you had money. Some sort of trust. You've taken several vacations already. God knows what they cost. And the cars!"

"You're correct, Mary Elizabeth. I bought each of us a new car and I have taken two vacations without you. I'd be willing to take two vacations with you if you were any kind of good company, but I will not pay for you to spend a year abroad."

"You fucking son-of-a-bitch!" Now she was screaming. She picked up a book that was on the table and threw it at me. Churchill growled at her and she stopped as if struck by some spell. "You better get that dog of yours under control."

"Actually, my dear Mary Elizabeth, you better get yourself under control." I noticed Mackenzie peeking around a corner.

"It's alright Mackenzie, Mommy and I are just arguing. We'll get it settled," I said. "Arguing is a normal thing. No reason to be afraid."

Mary Elizabeth grabbed her coat from the coat tree next to the front door and left. I picked Mackenzie up in my arms and held her. I put a record on and danced with her. Mama Cass sang, "I call your name…." Mackenzie quickly fell asleep and I was certain it was because she feared what she had heard and seen.

Something had to be done.

As usual, Mary Elizabeth returned sometime in the early hours of the morning. I had not gone to bed.

"Oh, you're still up," she said when she noticed me sitting on the sofa.

"Yes, I'm still up."

"You sound menacing."

"Good, I'm glad you noticed, because I am through putting up with your shit."

"Really. And just what do you intend to do about it?"

"I'm going to make that a surprise," I said.

"Fuck you," she said and went to bed.

I slept on the couch, but the following morning I told Mary Elizabeth I wanted her out of the apartment within a month. "Here is the thing dear girl, if you get out, I'll give you twenty-five thousand dollars toward your year in Europe. I will not pay you alimony, and I will have custody of Mackenzie. If you refuse this offer, I'll see to it that you are dead before the year is out."

"I'm calling the police. You think you can get away with this?"

"Please, call them. I'll deny that I ever made any threat. I'll say you are mentally unstable and of course we know that there are medical records to substantiate this. I'll say you are an unfit mother, that you leave Mackenzie and forget to pick her up, that you bully me because you had to take care of her while I served my country, was wounded, and became a war hero. I'll tell them you refused to visit me when I was hospitalized in Hawaii. Do you see the picture you've painted with your sick selfish actions, dear girl?"

She sat motionless, her eyes focused on the floor. "Would you really do that to me—kill me?"

"I would. And I'd tell them that your father knew what an unreliable selfish bitch you are and so left his money to me when he died. It all adds up, Mary Elizabeth."

She took her coat off the coat tree by the door and was about to leave, again. "I wouldn't leave right now," I said. "I've been keeping a log of all your walk-outs. All the times you simply take off and make no effort to check on Mackenzie's safety and well-being. I have enough to easily prove you a selfish unfit mother. Leave now and it goes in the log. And understand, I have already consulted a lawyer and a child psychiatrist at Columbia. I have already laid the ground work to make this happen."

And I had. I visited Dr. Steinway again. He knew about Mary Elizabeth. I had said I was concerned Mary Elizabeth might be suicidal and possibly having a lesbian affair. I scheduled two sessions with him trying to find a path for myself given the behavior of this woman I had married because she seduced me and got pregnant. He knew the story, her aversion to sex. Dr.

Marvin Steinway remembered her previous therapy because of this problem and how she stopped seeing him. I also saw an attorney whom I knew from my time in the military. Leon Silberg was a Harvard law graduate. He also was a very good friend. I had consulted with him several months before to set the stage for ridding myself of Mary Elizabeth without losing Mackenzie or a lot of money. He advised me well on what would be necessary to prove Mary Elizabeth unfit.

She put her coat back on the coat tree and walked quietly to the bedroom. I did not see her again until mid-afternoon when she emerged and asked if I wanted to shower. She sounded odd—detached or lethargic.

"What's wrong with you?" I asked. "Have you taken something? A sedative? Have you been drinking?" I made sure to sound very concerned and serious.

"I'm fine. I have a lot on my mind. I have to plan my life—the rest of my life. I've lost everything," she said and began to tremble.

"So far dear girl you haven't lost anything except me. What else you lose will depend on you and your choices." I turned to pick up the blanket I had used on the couch and as I leaned forward to gather it up, I sensed Mary Elizabeth moving toward me. As I looked up I saw she was moving quickly and her right arm was extended above her head. A pair of scissors were in her right hand and it looked as if she meant to stab me with them. I allowed her to make the thrust but then moved enough to deflect the blades away and toward my left arm. I wanted her to cut me, but not to disable me in any permanent manner.

She was not a strong woman. The blades left a four inch cut in my left forearm which was bleeding heavily. I quickly neutralized her and wrapped her in the blanket, using duct tape which I kept in my tool closet to immobilize her. I then called the police and reported that my wife had attempted to kill me. I made sure that I had bled well onto the floor and the rug before applying a tourniquet and a towel to act as a dressing.

While awaiting the police I called my parents and they were on the way to pick up Mackenzie. She was in her room with Churchill, whom I had to call off when Mary Elizabeth stabbed me. He was about to attack her. When the police arrived, I let them in. One officer remembered me as an ER physician at Harlem Hospital Center.

"Holy shit, Doc, is all this blood yours?"

"Yes. I didn't expect the attack. She came out of the bedroom and attacked me with those scissors." I pointed to the scissors which I had left on the floor.

"He tried to kill me!" Mary Elizabeth screamed and tried to thrash about in the blanket, but I had done a good job with the duct tape. "He's a murderer. He's going to kill me." She was shrieking and I heard Mackenzie begin to cry in her room.

"My parents are on the way here to pick up my daughter. I think my wife is going to need emergency psychiatric treatment. She has a psychiatrist," I said.

"Where is he?" one of the policemen asked.

"He practices at Columbia Presbyterian Medical Center, uptown. His name is Dr. Marvin Steinway."

"Oh you fucking bastard," Mary Elizabeth screamed.

"Please, I need to comfort my daughter," I said to the police. I walked quickly into Mackenzie's room and picked her up. She leaned forward and collapsed onto my right shoulder. I was able to hold her steady with my right arm. "It's okay Sweetheart, Mommy is upset. She needs to go to the hospital where the doctors can help her."

"Are they good doctors, Daddy?"

"They're the best, Mackenzie."

Two weeks later, I filled for divorce. My petition included mental cruelty, physical cruelty, and an offering for supervised visitation. Mary Elizabeth was still under forced commitment in the mental ward at Presbyterian Medical Center. Dr. Steinway considered her dangerous to herself and others. He called me in during her first few days of hospitalization and informed me that she was probably suffering from psychosis and had disassociated due to some serious past experience. I had asked if being raped as a child could be the cause. He had looked at me for a moment and then indicated that she may have lied to me about being raped. He said no more other than that she needed to be in the hospital and medicated for a while longer.

A week later, he called me back to his office. "I'm afraid we are not making progress. She says you set her up for all of this; that you mean to kill her. She seems terribly paranoid, or perhaps she has reason to be if in fact you did threaten her." He stopped speaking and looked at me.

"Look Dr. Steinway, I have many reasons to despise this woman. You know our history. But, I would never hurt her. I might want her out of my life, because she is such a destructive force for me and for our daughter. But I'm not a fool. I have a wonderful life. Why would I want to jeopardize that by killing anyone? I've done enough killing for my country. I would never lay a hand on Mary Elizabeth. She's my daughter's mother."

He looked at me again for a moment, definitely sizing up the voracity of my statement. I'm not certain he was buying it, but he shook his head as if to concur. "But did you threaten her—perhaps in anger?"

"I may have said something metaphorically. Sometimes when I'm angry with her I may say that I'd like to kill her, but I've never said it in earnest and she knows that."

"Maybe she doesn't, Michael," he said. "Why don't we sit with her together and you tell her that. I want to see how she reacts to you."

His office was in the hospital complex. We took an elevator and went to her room. The orderly unlocked the door. There were two chairs in the room, and Dr. Steinway moved them to the right side of Mary Elizabeth's bed. When she saw me enter the room she pulled the thin woven hospital blanket up to her neck and had a terrified helpless look. I considered that she was acting the part of a poor helpless terrified wife. How would I play my part? Who would be more believable?

"Mary Elizabeth, I'm so sorry if I frightened you. I've never hurt you. I've always protected you." I walked over to her bed and attempted to lean over and hug her.

She pulled away and thrust herself up against the metal headboard, staring at me with hateful eyes. There were no tears. Perhaps it was the medications she was being given.

"Mary Elizabeth, Michael doesn't want to hurt you. He wants to help you, but if you continue to behave as you are, no good will come of it. You can't stab people because they frighten you," Dr. Steinway said.

I had to hope that between the medication, some degree of mental instability which she undoubtedly harbored—she had attempted to kill me—and my new approach to send her off the edge, I'd be able to get her out of my life. I had in addition to the divorce filing, also filed a restraining order, which had been certified by the court. Mary Elizabeth tried to kill me! I continued to behave in a sad but helpful manner.

"He's going to kill me," she screamed. "He said he was going to kill me. I had to protect myself." She was trembling and crying.

Bravo, Mary Elizabeth, I thought, but I said, "Please, let me help you."

She looked at me again and Dr. Steinway could see the wild hatred in her eyes. I think she knew that I had her. It took a special degree of coldness and patience to play my role. I was good at it. It would exact revenge. I was certain Mary Elizabeth had tricked me into marrying her. She had ruined enough of my life. Now, I was close to absolute zero and quietly patient. Yes, she knew that I had her.

EPILOGUE

EPILOGUE

In December of 1972, Mary Elizabeth was discharged to a halfway house in Greenwich Village. She switched her studies to NYU. The divorce was granted and the restraining order maintained. There was a modest alimony payment but I had custody of Mackenzie. As each month passed I think her hatred for me grew greater. She was only permitted to see Mackenzie under the supervision of a social worker for several hours once a month.

"Daddy, what happened to Mommy?" Mackenzie had asked. "I don't think she likes me. Is that why she can't live here anymore?"

I knew the situation was fuel for some serious problems as Mackenzie grew older. I also knew it might affect our relationship when she grew up if I didn't handle the loss of her mother carefully.

"Mommy isn't a nice person," I said. "She thinks of herself before anyone else and usually people who do that don't know how to love. It isn't a good thing, Mackenzie, and I'm sorry you have to feel sad. I don't know why Mommy isn't a nice person. She also doesn't care about me. She tried to hurt me."

"I know, Daddy, I saw what she did to you. I was watching from my bedroom. Churchill didn't like it either. But sometimes, she was nice to me, Daddy. She must have loved me a little."

Yes, there it was; the seed of future trouble for Mackenzie. I knew it would be largely up to me to try to get that seed out before it grew deep roots. It was a rainy March morning. I had the day off and planned on spending it with Mackenzie. I believed in telling the truth to children, but I didn't want to overload my little daughter with more truth than she was prepared to process at her age. I often thought my mother had done this to me.

"I think she did love you in her own way. But then her not-nice behavior can take charge and make her mean. That's why she can't see you without someone else being there to protect you."

"Would she try to hurt me?"

"I don't know, Mackenzie, but I'm not willing to take a chance on it."

"Should I keep seeing her, Daddy?"

"As long as you are never alone with her. It makes good sense to be safe."

She looked at me for a moment and then sat down beside Churchill, who was curled up on his rug beside my chair. She leaned over and laid her head on the big white dog. He thumped his tail several times on the floor, lifted his head to look at her and took a deep breath of the cool air in the apartment.

As days became longer and warmer, Mackenzie, Churchill and I spent many hours playing in Central Park. Churchill loved to retrieve a tennis ball. He could play at this for hours. Mackenzie couldn't throw very far, so it was usually she who wore out first.

Sometimes I'd rent a row boat on the lake and take Mackenzie and Churchill for a boat ride. We shared good times in the Park.

I also thought Mackenzie was getting old enough to take on a vacation. We went to Disney World in Florida. It seemed to provide an excellent distraction for my daughter.

Shortly after our return, I was contacted and made another visit to Abercrombie and Fitch. The routine was similar except this time I'd have a new identity complete with passport and driver's license and the new mission was unlike previous ones. This exercise would not involve assassination. The plan called for a September departure to the Caribbean. Jim also warned me that some of Wojinoska's people were snooping around. The agency had planted the story that the expensive consort who accompanied him was a hired Russian assassin. Apparently, some of his former associates were not buying that story.

Mary Elizabeth continued to see Mackenzie one weekend each month. Mackenzie seemed agitated whenever a visiting weekend arrived.

"Daddy, do I have to see Momma?"

"I think you should. I think that one day you will be glad you did."

"But Daddy, I don't like the way she touches me."

"I don't understand."

"Her hands are always wet and cold, and she shakes. It's scary."

I thought it might be one of the medications Mary Elizabeth was taking. It concerned me and I discussed this with my attorney.

"What if it isn't medication? What if she is agitated because she intends to harm Mackenzie?" I said.

My lawyer, Leon, didn't say anything for a moment. He stared out the window with his hands folded as if in prayer and his fingertips softly tapping against his lips. Then he stood up and paced in front of the large office window, which overlooked the upper east side of Manhattan and the East River. The Queensboro Bridge was in view, and portions of the towers of the Manhattan and Williamsburg Bridges could also be seen. The office was on the 60th floor of the Chrysler Building and gave a clear view of an Eagle Gargoyle several floors above. I was looking at sunlight flashing off the chrome shell of the Eagle's head and neck, wondering how I could protect my daughter from the beast who was her mother.

"Look, we have to stop this," he said after the long pause. "Your ex-wife seems dangerous enough to be a serious potential harm to your daughter. I need to think about it. See if there have been other legal precedents that we might use to our advantage. I was concerned about Mackenzie losing her mother, but now I think the risks far outweigh the benefits. Give me a week to investigate alternatives and I'll get back to you," Leon said.

We shook hands on it and I left. I trusted Leon Silberg. He had been a good soldier. We never really fought together because he was not part of the special warfare teams, but my team had helped rescue his infantry platoon when they were trapped in a South Vietnamese village by an NVA unit. His platoon had taken heavy losses and he fought bravely and doggedly to keep the NVA unit at bay until my team arrived to distract and harass the enemy so helicopters could get in and extract his people. We met after that at a debriefing and I liked what I saw. After, we stayed in touch. He was in law school while I attended medical school. He would never accept any money from me. He always referred to a debt he could not repay. Although I didn't see it that way, I accepted his kindness. On one occasion when we had been recalling that day in the jungle, he said, "Those NVA regulars were picking us apart. I thought it was over. Then all hell broke loose and I figured an infantry company had come to our rescue. I still don't understand how five guys can cause such an illusion." I told him it was the helicopter gunships that raised most of the hell. But I didn't tell him how a five man Special Warfare team could in-fact create illusions. That was an operational secret.

My idea about how to do away with Mary Elizabeth was also an operational secret. I discussed it with no one. But from time to time I couldn't help thinking about the objective as I would a mission. It had to be clean and fast and leave no indication or evidence that I was responsible. I thought about this because I truly feared the impact a mentally unstable and hateful mother would have upon Mackenzie. But I was more than ambivalent about the idea. The same question kept coming up in my mind: How would I ever be able to look my daughter in the eye as she grew up, knowing I had killed her mother? I certainly knew better than to anticipate hiring anyone else to do the job—a sure fire way of being found out. No, if such a deed were to be done it had to be done by me.

One evening I was convincing myself of all the reasons why I could not remove Mary Elizabeth from this planet when the phone rang.

Leon had not yet called about his thoughts to legally remove Mary Elizabeth's harmful influence on Mackenzie. It was around 9pm on a hot Monday evening in July. I picked up the receiver. "Hello, Michael Ross," I said. I thought it might be Leon. He often called me after hours to discuss the legal matters pertaining to Mary Elizabeth and me.

"Yes, are you Dr. Michael Ross?"

"I am. Who is this?"

"Dr. Ross, this is Sergeant Rydle. I'm a New York City police detective. Is Mary Elizabeth Ross your wife?

"My ex-wife," I said, trying to keep my voice as steady as I could because I suspected no good news. "What has she done now?"

"I received a call from someone named Eleanor LaRouche. She's apparently a friend of your wife's."

"Ex-wife," I added.

"Okay, ex-wife. When did you last see her or hear from her?"

"There is a restraining order keeping her away from me. I haven't seen her in over a month. And I never communicate with her."

"Okay, but here's the thing, we found her purse and credit cards on some street junky down around the NYU campus. The Eleanor woman says she hasn't heard from this Mary Elizabeth person in days and suggested we call you."

"Well, Eleanor and Mary Elizabeth were very good friends. They attended NYU together in a graduate program, Columbia and Fordham before that. I can't help here, but please understand that Mary Elizabeth O'Rourke and I have a child—a four year old girl. I have custody. My daughter sees her mother once a month in a visit supervised by a social worker. The last visit was three weeks ago."

"Look Doc, can I come to your home and talk to you. I also would like you to confirm the purse and wallet as belonging to your wife—ex-wife."

"When would you like to come over?"

"How about tomorrow morning?"

"Fine. I'm off tomorrow." I gave the detective my address.

Detective Rydle showed up at nine the next morning. He was a short bald man in a worn brown sport jacket and beige chinos. He had a plastic bag with him. It contained a purse, a wallet, and some credit cards. I actually remembered when she bought the wallet. It was red. I watched her fill out the ID card. She had put Eleanor's name and number as the emergency contact person, which had pissed me off at the time.

"Yes, that looks like Mary Elizabeth's wallet. I don't recognize the purse. The credit cards obviously have her name on them."

The detective put on rubber gloves and removed the wallet from the plastic bag. He opened it and showed me a picture of Mackenzie, one of Churchill, and one of her with her father that was quite old. I had never seen it.

"That is our daughter and her father," I said pointing at but not touching the respective pictures. "And that is my dog, Churchill." I had left him in Mackenzie's room and when I said his name he barked.

"Sounds like a big dog," Rydle said.

"Want to meet him?" I asked.

"No, I'm not crazy about big dogs and they always seem to sense it. You know I did some snooping about you and you had quite a military career. An airborne ranger. Combat wounded. Now you work for Columbia University at the Harlem ER."

"All correct information."

"You don't seem too upset about this situation with your Ex."

"I don't wear my feelings on the outside," I said.

"It isn't a good thing when we discover this kind of a situation."

"I'm sure it isn't. Do you think she may be dead?"

"Very likely. Maybe in a dumpster someplace. We'll keep looking. Why the restraining order?" he added.

I looked at him for a moment because if he investigated me, he knew why. He didn't turn his eyes away from mine. "I'm sure you already know the answer to that. She stabbed me. She accused me of threatening to kill her. She was mentally unstable and still is."

"Unless she is dead. Did you kill her Dr. Ross?"

"What do you think Detective Rydle?" I kept my focus on his eyes.

"I'll be in touch if we find anything," he said and left.

Three weeks later they found one of her shoes in a dumpster awaiting a barge trip out to the Atlantic dumping site for NY City. They searched all the rest of the garbage but found nothing until one of the dump crews discovered a decomposing body afloat at sea when another barge's load was tossed overboard. It turned out to be Mary Elizabeth's body. Rydle had called with the news and I had to identify the body, which was near impossible. They finally used dental records. I felt some sorrow for her, but also some relief for myself and my daughter. The coroner confirmed death by a blow to the head. There was no evidence of rape, but with all the decomposition, the coroner said it was impossible to be sure. The final disposition of the case was a mugging and murder, and the junky who had her purse was charged. He swore he found it in the same dumpster where they found her shoe. Nonetheless, he took a plea bargain for manslaughter in the commission of a robbery to avoid a possible death sentence or life in prison. He got twenty years.

I had the remains cremated and bought an inexpensive box for the ashes. I placed it on a shelf in the library—all that was left of Mary Elizabeth. Churchill raised his nose to the box one time and sniffed with characteristic intent. He stood for a moment longer, staring at the box, ears keen, then walked off to his favorite corner and went to sleep. Mary Elizabeth's family heard about the murder on TV. They contacted me. I told them she had been cremated. I wanted nothing to do with them. I disposed of the ashes off the Jersey Shore. Her family loved the Jersey Shore. Eleanor never contacted me, nor I her.

Mrs. Floric brought occasional casserole meals, and each time she rang the doorbell, Mackenzie would ask if it was her mother. I told her that her mother had died. I said she was sick and died. I wasn't ready to give her the gruesome details at only four years of age.

My mother and sometimes my dad as well, came to stay with us whenever I worked an ER shift. I took off only for one week after the killing or robbery or whatever it was. Mother was probably saddest of all. She spoke to me about her sorrow—Mackenzie growing up without a mother.

I was not sad. Not even a little sad. Mary Elizabeth had made my life miserable. I was glad to be rid of her, considered myself lucky that providence had, somehow, worked in my favor. Mackenzie would have plenty of love and attention. She would be fine—perhaps even better off without Mary Elizabeth's self-pity filled perspective.

During the month of August, I took another week off. Mackenzie and I flew to Paris for five days. I carried her up and down the Champs Elise on my shoulders, whenever she tired of walking. We played in the Tuileries Gardens and walked through the Louvre. She enjoyed the pictures and the attention from lovely young women. One of the stewardesses on the Pan Am flight was particularly lovely and based in New York City. I asked her to join me for dinner some evening in the City and got her phone number before we landed.

Everyone thought that I needed time to recover from the shock and the loss, but I didn't. In fact, happiness filled my days, again. It felt grand to not awaken most mornings filled with hatred. Nonetheless, I would say to friends and family that I did not understand why life chose to end Mary Elizabeth's existence. I would say that I had to heal and that life must go on for Mackenzie and me. We had experienced terrible stress and emotional trauma because of Mary Elizabeth O'Rourke, and now she was gone and we were free of her.

Perhaps my escaping the undertow back in '48 was somehow prophetic. After all, had my oldest older sister and brother-in-law not come along, I may well have felt the need to challenge the warning from the lifeguard and my parents. It was in my nature to challenge things—just as it is in my nature to want to relieve suffering and remove the scum who make the world a lesser place through their unreasonable and harmful choices. So, being spared from a young death may have been for a purpose.

Yes, it's easy for me to take charge. Of course, my life has not gone exactly as I would have liked, but whose does? What is important is that I was able to get things back on track. So far,

I'd give myself an A-minus, but it isn't over till it is. I was looking forward to the Caribbean in September—just two weeks away.

L

Back in the ER working my usual shifts, five of them before I would leave for Jamaica, I had convinced the chief of medicine that I was ready to resume my job. "I need to get back to my life," I had said, "if I am going to heal."

On my first shift back, a woman in her thirties came in by ambulance covered in her own blood. The story we got was that her husband found her fucking another man. He shot and killed the other man and then placed the shotgun in his wife's vagina and pulled the trigger. She was probably not going to live, but at the moment she was alive and the OB- GYN team and the general surgical team were working on her, desperately attempting the impossible; to save her life. Her pelvic cavity and lower abdomen were in shards and blood was leaking out of her faster than the three transfusion lines could replace it.

As this scene was unfolding, I saw a man in an overcoat walk very intently into the ER. Security in those days was more after than before the fact. I could see the tip of a shotgun barrel sticking out from beneath his coat. I walked slowly toward him as he quietly moved down the central corridor of the ER. He was looking into treatment rooms. I considered this might be the husband looking to finish the job on his apparently unfaithful wife. I approached him from behind as he was coming up to the cubical where his dying wife was being treated. I did not want to confront him in a manner that would allow him to use the shotgun on me or others in the ER. Just as I reached him he slipped the shotgun from under his coat and began to raise it to fire at his wife and the team working over her. It was a semi-automatic 12 gauge. I came over his head with my arms and forced the shotgun down toward the floor. He did manage to pull the trigger, but the buckshot drilled into the vinyl tiles and marble on the floor. He was a big fellow so I quickly broke his neck as he was trying to raise the gun again. He collapsed dead to the floor , the team in the cubical looking toward me with open mouths and fear-filled eyes.

"Jesus Christ All Mighty," Kanzer the head ER nurse said. "He could have killed us."

A security guard and then a uniformed police officer arrived on the run. The officer pushed the shotgun away. There was another round of double 0 buck shot in the chamber, which the officer removed. The security guard and the officer both re-holstered their side-arms.

"Where the hell did you learn to do that?" the officer asked me.

"I was an Army Ranger before I was a physician," I said.

"Christ Doc, you broke his neck."

"He was going to kill more people with that weapon," I said. "I had to stop him. The idea was to get the shotgun out of his hands without having him pull the trigger again."

That was my story and I stuck to it. There was a coroner's inquest, and the shooters family even threatened to sue me and the hospital for excessive use of force and wrongful death. The inquest found my actions justified and the family's civil case never got off the ground because the coroner said I had to use deadly force to save lives and probably broke his neck by accident. Everyone agreed that had I not solved the problem, more innocent people would have been killed. The fact that I had been trained in the art of neck-breaking during my days at Hurlbert never surfaced. At the time, the secrecy surrounding black ops was superior and no one had any idea that I was a CIA asset. That information did not exist—anywhere.

The night before I was to leave on my next job, I took Mackenzie and Churchill to my parents' home. My mother told me Lovey Cohen had called. She left a number and asked that I get in touch with her. I didn't call her that night. I had to keep my mind on my mission. I hugged Mackenzie and kissed her. She hugged me back but was more interested in playing with her grandpa. I returned to my New York apartment in the Corvette. I had rented garage space for it in a neighboring building's private garage. I could now afford the convenience. I went to bed early and had a bizarre dream.

I was standing on a beach. The sand was cold. There was a wall of sea-fog at the waters edge. I could see a shadow-like form just within the fog, a headless body standing in the bow of a very small boat. Only the bow of the boat was visible. The headless body-shadow held an infant by the ankle—held it up so I could see what it was.

"You," the shadow said.

"Me?" I said. And wondered where the sound was coming from since the body-shadow had no head.

"No, you," it repeated and threw the infant at me.

I awoke with a start. Took a cold shower and called a cab to take me to the airport.